W9-AHH-185

Withdrawn

WHO STOLE
NEW YEAR'S EVE?

THE CHICKADEE COURT MYSTERIES

WHO STOLE
NEW YEAR'S EVE?

MARTHA FREEMAN

CHICKADEE COURT MYSTERY #5

Holiday House / New York

This book was inspired by biofuel research at Pennsylvania
State University and elsewhere, by the boom in hydraulic fracturing
for natural gas extraction in Pennsylvania, and by the annual First Night
celebration in State College. While there may be similarities in the
chemicals used for fracking and those used in the development
of biofuels, most of the chemistry in this book is fictional.

Text copyright © 2013 by Martha Freeman
All Rights Reserved
HOLIDAY HOUSE is registered in the U.S. Patent and Trademark Office.
Printed and bound in July 2013 at Maple Press, York, PA, USA.
First Edition
1 3 5 7 9 10 8 6 4 2
www.holidayhouse.com

Library of Congress Cataloging-in-Publication Data

Freeman, Martha, 1956–
Who stole New Year's Eve? Martha Freeman. — 1st ed.
p. cm. — (A Chickadee Court mystery)
Summary: Sixth-grader Alex and his friend Yasmeen are on the case when ice
sculptures go missing from the local First Night festivities.
ISBN 978-0-8234-2750-5 (hardcover)
[1. Mystery and detective stories.   2. Ice carving—Fiction.
3. Carnivals—Fiction.   4. Pennsylvania—Fiction.]   I. Title.
PZ7.F87496Wjm 2013
[Fic]—dc23
2012019674

CHAPTER ONE

The first time I ever saw Eve Henry, I was holding a chocolate cream pie.

Her family had just moved into the house down the street. I rang the doorbell, Eve answered, and her face lit up. I wanted to believe the smile was on account of my good looks. But it was probably on account of the pie.

"Hello, I'm Alex Parakeet," I said. "I'm in sixth grade. My mom and dad sent the pie and me over to welcome your family to the neighborhood."

That speech might not sound like much, but I had practiced it twice so I wouldn't mess up.

"Oh, wow, thanks." Eve took the pie. "I'm Eve Henry. I'm from California, and I'm in seventh grade. Do you want to come in and meet my mom?"

I didn't know how to tell Eve no, so I sort of said, "Unhhh," and then Eve explained that it was only she and her mom at home. Her dad was at work. He was a new professor at the college, and he was busy setting up his lab.

Actually, I already knew Eve's dad was a professor.

The people on my street, Chickadee Court, had found out a couple of weeks ago that new neighbors were moving into the Dagostinos' old house, and it didn't take long for the details to spread: They were from California, and Eve was an only child; her mom had grown up in Belleburg, Pennsylvania, which is over the mountain from us here in College Springs.

Besides being a professor, Eve's dad supposedly had some big scientific idea that might change the world. The college was paying him a lot of money and building a big, expensive lab for his research.

What was his big idea? That remained a mystery.

"Please come in, Alex," Eve said. "I don't know any kids yet, and I'm sick of unpacking boxes." With that, Eve turned and went back inside, leaving the front door open. What could I do? I went in.

I have been in the Dagostinos' house plenty of times, but now it looked strange. There were boxes everywhere and different furniture. In the kitchen, a lady who had to be Mrs. Henry was kneeling on the floor, cleaning out a cupboard. "Who was at the door, sweetie?" she asked without looking around.

"Alex, uh...what's your last name again?" Eve asked.

"Parakeet," I said. "Alex Parakeet."

Mrs. Henry sat up—"Oh, dear, so sorry. I didn't

2

see you!"—and got to her feet. Like her daughter, she had straight white teeth and blond hair, the way you'd expect on somebody from California.

"A Parakeet on Chickadee Court?" Mrs. Henry said. "That should be easy to remember." She wiped her hand on her jeans, then held it out. "I'm Jessica Henry."

"It's nice to meet you, Mrs. Henry," I said.

Mrs. Henry noticed the pie and fussed about how nice I was to bring it over.

"My dad made it," I explained. "Making pies is his job now."

"And I think it's your dad who put up the five gold rings for us, too." Mrs. Henry was talking about the Christmas display. Every year the people on our street decorate their houses to go with the "Twelve Days of Christmas" song. We're the seventh house, so we're seven swans a-swimming. Two houses over, the Henrys are five gold rings—and last week my dad, along with some other neighbors, put up the spray-painted Hula-Hoops so they wouldn't have to.

"My dad helped," I said. And then, I think because I was a little uncomfortable, I kept right on talking. I explained how my mom was a police detective, the only one in College Springs, and how my dad didn't have a paying job for a long time because he had been taking care of me and the house, but this fall he started a pie baking business.

For me, this was already a lot of talking, but Mrs. Henry smiled and nodded so much that I also told her about some of the neighbors, like the Jensens, who host the annual holiday party; and Bub, who lives in a small house and makes good soup and bad coffee for anybody who stops by; and Sophie Sikora, who is a year younger than me and a loud-mouth and some kind of electronics genius.

"I'm looking forward to meeting them all," Mrs. Henry said. "And the party is tonight, right?"

I nodded. "Pretty much everyone goes, too—except this year my mom can't. She's busy with work."

Eve's eyes widened. "You mean like she has to catch a *murderer*?"

I smiled. "Nothing like that. Somebody's been phoning in tips to the police department, and she has to investigate."

Eve's mom said she'd always heard College Springs was pretty safe.

I said, "Most of the time it is," but I was thinking how actually a few bad things do happen—like last summer when my baseball coach got temporarily kidnapped. But before I could explain that, I heard *Arf! Arf! Arf!,* then toenails scrabbling against

4

wood. Next thing you know, a white dust-mop of a dog bounded in from the hallway, pop-eyed and panting.

Eve still had the pie in her hands, which turned out to be unfortunate because right away the dust mop forgot his fear, homed in on it, and sprang. Quick on her feet, Eve dodged so that the dog missed, but then she stumbled against the open cupboard door and the dog sprang again—bull's-eye!

Mayday! Mayday! The pie was goin' down. En route, it did a slo-mo 360, but—amazingly—I managed to snag the edge of the pan. For a second I thought I'd saved the day, then—oh, heartbreak—the pie broke free and crash-landed—*splat*. The pan was still in my hand, but what had been dessert was now crust and goo—tasty crust and goo, I guess, because the dust-mop dog was all over it, not to mention that it was all over him, a chocolate-and-pie-crust mud bath.

"*Bad dog! Bad!*" Mrs. Henry scolded.

"Get away from there, pup." Eve knelt and shoved him back. "Chocolate's bad for you!"

Arf! Arf! Arf! the little guy argued, which meant *How can something be bad if it tastes good?*

After that, there was a flurry of cleanup activity—the dog, the floor, the pie's remains—and I figured my job was to stay out of the way.

"I never saw that kind of dog before," I said after Eve had finished wiping pie off his face. "What is he?"

"Mostly Maltese," Eve said. "They're very popular where I used to live in California. His name's Marshmallow."

"Hey, guy." I reached to scratch behind his ears; he licked my hand. "He likes me."

"He likes everybody," Eve said, "except—" From the hall doorway came a loud *mrrree-ow* that overlapped Eve's last word—"cats."

When we looked toward the sound we saw a very large orange feline who—I happen to know—is totally happy to terrorize dogs when he gets the chance.

Mrs. Henry spoke to the cat. "Where did you come from?"

And I said, "Sorry, uh…he's mine; I guess he followed me from home then sneaked in the door behind me." I crossed my arms over my chest and looked stern. "Way to go, Luau—scaring the new neighbor."

Luau ducked his nose and swished his tail, which meant, *Can I help it if he overreacted?*

Eve looked first at Luau then at me. "Uh… Alex? Are you talking to your cat?"

Oops. I tried to act casual. "Uh, sure," I said.

"Like everybody does. You know, 'Nice kitty,' 'Good kitty.' 'Fat kitty....'"

Luau wiped a paw over his whiskers. *Fat?*

"I'd better take him home," I said, "before he causes any more trouble."

At the door, Eve thanked me for coming over. "Now I'll know one person at the party tonight, at least."

"I'll introduce you to Yasmeen, my best friend who happens to be a girl," I said. "Her family's eight maids a-milking, next door to my house. Maybe you've seen her?"

"The tall African American girl?" Eve asked.

I nodded. "Her family's from Trinidad. She's really smart. You guys're gonna get along great."

CHAPTER TWO

The Jensens' annual holiday party starts just after dark, which is around four-thirty in December, and every year it's the same. The grown-ups hang out upstairs in the living room, and the kids stay downstairs in the basement. There are two Christmas trees, two fireplaces, twinkle lights everywhere, eggnog, snacks, and a million cookies.

The highlight comes at eight o'clock when Professor Jensen flips a switch to turn on the lights and music for the twelve-day display all down Chickadee Court. By then, people from all over have come to watch. Outside on the sidewalk, they whistle and applaud.

My dad had had some last-minute pie orders to fill, so the Jensens' house was full of people by the time we arrived. After Professor Jensen welcomed us and took our coats, Mrs. Henry—standing by the fancy white Christmas tree in the living room—spotted me, smiled, and waved me over. Next to her was a tall man with curly gray hair and glasses. It had to be her husband, Professor Henry, and this was my chance to solve the mystery of his big idea. Only, I had to wait because he was busy talking to Yasmeen's dad.

Since they're both professors, their conversation was super-brainy, and I couldn't exactly follow it, but one thing was obvious: They weren't getting along at all!

Mrs. Henry shrugged at me and looked embarrassed and finally interrupted: "*Dear?* I told you about Alex?"

The two professors had been glaring at each other. Now they looked down and glared at me.

"Hi," I said in a small voice.

Mrs. Henry explained about the welcome pie and how I'm almost the same age as Eve. Slowly, Professor Henry's frown faded, and then he said nice to meet you and thanks anyway for the pie.

I said, "You're welcome," then did my best to sound jolly and enthusiastic the way grown-ups do at parties. "So, Professor Henry, what brings your family to College Springs? Are you doing any interesting work at the college?"

Professor Henry opened his mouth to respond, but before he could, Mrs. Popp came up and held her hand out to him. "I don't believe we've met."

Uh-oh. Now it was up to me to introduce them to each other. I mean, I was the only one who knew all the names. So I tried, but I got confused and actually introduced Mrs. Popp to her own husband. Oops.

Everybody laughed; I blushed, and for the next few minutes boring grown-up chitchat hummed above my head. Then it stopped, and when I looked up, four pairs of eyes were aimed at my face.

"Wait, what?" I said. "Sorry. I forgot to listen. I mean—"

Mrs. Popp laughed. "Our new neighbors were just saying, Alex, that their daughter Eve's birthday is next weekend—on New Year's Day, in fact. She's hoping to have a get-together the day before. I'm sure you and Yasmeen could plan to attend? And perhaps encourage the other children?"

"Uh, sure," I said. "We usually go to Ice Carnival, but—"

"Oh, that's right!" said Mrs. Henry. "How could I have forgotten? My brother's a sculptor who lives over the mountain in Belleburg. In the winter he works in ice, and the carnival is his most important contract. Tell you what, how about if the kids come over after Carnival? We could have a New Year's Eve party to celebrate Eve's birthday."

"Wow, that would be great!" I said. "Usually I hate New Year's Eve because all the grown-ups go to parties and there's nothing for me to do."

Professor Popp wagged his finger. "There is good reason for that, my young friend. It is not a holiday for children. Your parents, I am sure, would never permit you to be out so late."

"Oh, come on," said Mrs. Henry. "Staying up one night a year never hurt anybody."

The stern expression on Professor Popp's face said he thought staying up one night a year would, too, hurt somebody; it might even be fatal. Meanwhile, Professor Henry said, "Hmph. I didn't realize people in College Springs were such goody-goods."

Uh-oh. Were they going to start arguing again?

I didn't stick around to find out.

Instead, I excused myself and went downstairs to hang with the kids. In the basement, Toby Lee and Cammie Richmond were trying to strangle each other with tinsel, but that was just usual. Meanwhile, there were two TVs going, one with video games and one with *A Charlie Brown Christmas*, and a bunch of food on a table in the middle of the room—three kinds of chips, Hershey's Kisses, Christmas cookies with white icing, brownies, and Oreos. In a cooler on the floor were cans of Pepsi, Coke, and Orange Crush.

As I guess you can tell, the Jensens really know how to put on a party.

Eve Henry was by the food table. I was glad she

had found somebody to talk to—a black girl wearing a red dress and shiny black shoes, her billowy hair pulled back with barrettes.

I was trying to decide which chips to eat first when the black girl waved.

Huh?

I looked around, looked back—and realized the girl was waving at *me*. Also, she wasn't just some random person—she was Yasmeen!

Sorry if you already figured that out. But Yasmeen only dresses up for church and she always wears her hair in braids. This new version of her was different—pretty.

That idea was so weird that I squelched it.

"Alex, you have the strangest expression on your face—doesn't he, Eve?" Yasmeen said.

Eve shrugged. "I thought that was just the way he always looks."

"I'm *fine*." I stuffed a handful of nacho chips in my mouth and crunched. "Hey, Eve—what's your dad's big scientific idea, anyway? I didn't have a chance to ask you today, so I was gonna ask him just now, but, uh…that didn't work out."

Eve blinked. "I'm not supposed to talk about it yet, I don't think. There's supposed to be an announcement in the newspaper."

Yasmeen cocked her head. "Ohhh, so it's some kind of a big deal, huh?"

Eve shrugged. "Where we lived in California, people thought so."

Now I was really curious, but Eve wasn't saying more, and then my friend Ari called me over to the sofa, where he was playing video games. I figured he wanted my advice on Lousy Luigi—I am pretty good at it—but it turned out to be something different.

"Who's the babe?" he asked, raising his eyebrows.

"The 'babe'?" I repeated. "You mean Eve?" This was almost as bad as Yasmeen being pretty.

"*Duh!*" said Sophie Sikora, who had leaned over to listen.

I skipped over the whole "babe" thing and explained about Eve, including her birthday and how there might be a party.

"Cool!" said Sophie. "What this town needs is something for kids to do on New Year's Eve."

"Can I come?" Ari lives around the corner.

"I don't know for sure if it's even happening," I said.

"Be right back," Sophie said, and she headed toward Eve. One thing about Sophie, she gets to the bottom of things.

I turned my focus to Lousy Luigi. The Jensens have the latest version, the one with a cannon for shooting oregano. My Luigi guy was knee-deep in cheese when Sophie came back.

"That new girl's pretty nice, and she says if it's okay with her parents, everybody's going to be invited—except for little kids like my brother Byron, of course."

Ari pumped his fist. "Yes!"

I handed him the game controller. I had an idea. "Sophie, could you help me with something?"

Sophie said, "Sure, and I hope it's another mystery because that would be totally great. Can I tell you how boring my life is lately? A girl can only get so much excitement out of math extra credit and fighting with her parents."

"It's a kind of a mystery." I explained how I was trying to find out Professor Henry's big idea.

"That's easy," said Sophie, and before I could even get to my feet, she was rocketing up the steps.

I caught up with her in the upstairs hall, just in time to hear the sharp thud of the front door closing and feel a blast of cold outside air. In the living room, the grown-ups were acting funny. Some were talking too loud and smiling too hard; some weren't talking at all.

Sophie turned to the nearest one. "Mrs. Ryan, what happened here?"

Mrs. Ryan—partridge in a pear tree—is a third-grade teacher and tough. "It's that new neighbor, Tom Henry I think his name is. He just walked out and slammed the door behind him."

So much for asking him about his idea.

"He had an argument"—Mrs. Ryan pointed—"with that gentleman over there. Do you know him? Enzo Olivo. He's a fossil fuels professor, knows all about oil and gas."

Next to the fireplace was a short man with a beard, dressed in a black suit and a red bow tie. It took a second, but then I realized he's friends with the Popps and I had seen him at their house before.

"Mrs. Ryan?" Sophie was all business. "Do you know what Professor Henry's big scientific idea is?"

Mrs. Ryan shook her head. "All I know about Professor Henry is that his social skills need work."

It was only seven-forty-five, but already a few people were by the front door getting their coats. "Hey everybody—please don't go." Mrs. Jensen waved them back into the living room. "What do you say we turn on the lights a little early?"

I wondered if anybody was out on the street

yet and reached across the sofa to pull open the drapes. A couple of cars were at the curb, and one family was walking on the sidewalk. There would be more people in a few minutes, but I could see why the Jensens wanted to hurry up. If we waited, there might not be any party left.

"Is everybody here?" Professor Jensen asked. "Have we got the kids from downstairs?"

Michael Jensen said, "All present and accounted for, Dad," and I noticed Yasmeen and Eve behind him.

"All right, then!" Professor Jensen flipped the switch, the outside lights blazed, and the music started: *"On the first day of Christmas, my true love gave to me…"*

Most of the grown-ups cringed. I guess the song does get kind of old. But after a verse, we were all singing along.

Party saved?

Not quite.

One voice rose above the rest. It wasn't a good voice, but it was loud: Yasmeen's.

Next to me Sophie giggled, and I elbowed her to cut it out. "She's trying really hard," I whispered. "She's even taking lessons so she can sing in her church choir."

Several people glanced at Yasmeen and smiled,

but she didn't notice; she was singing her heart out…until Eve, standing beside her, couldn't help it and erupted with a squawk of laughter so contagious it got everybody going. At first Yasmeen didn't realize she was the cause, but when she did, she shut her mouth and made a face so sad and terrible I felt it in my chest.

My poor friend.

I moved toward Yasmeen, not knowing how I was going to help, but before I could get near her, she had shouldered her way to the front door. She didn't even bother with her coat, just pulled the door open and walked out. Then, on the front step, she looked back and shot Eve a laser death stare worthy of my mom.

Ouch.

CHAPTER THREE

I got home a few minutes later. Mom was there already, sitting in the recliner in the den. She had a book on her tummy, and her eyes were closed. I said "Hello?" and she jumped.

"You were asleep," I said.

"Guilty as charged," she said. "What time is it? Where's your dad? Was it a fun party?"

"Whoa—I can't answer so many questions at once."

"Try," Mom said.

"Okay." I thought back. "It's around eight-thirty. Dad is helping the Jensens clean up. Uh...no, it was not a fun party. Singing lessons aren't helping Yasmeen. I tried to find out what big idea Professor Henry has, but I couldn't."

Mom's eyes had been blinking for a while, and now her chin dropped down on her chest. Meanwhile, Luau came in, jumped up on the arm of the recliner, butted Mom in the face, and looked at me: *This one's out cold, Alex. You know, she works too hard.*

"I do know." I petted my cat, and he arched his back. "Mom? Wake up. You need to go upstairs so you can go to sleep."

"Awea'y as'eep," she mumbled.

Luckily, I heard a noise in the front hall. Dad had come home. "Dad, come in here and deal with Mom, would you?"

Dad looked at her and shook his head. "Noreen, Noreen, Noreen—I thought we agreed at Thanksgiving? You're supposed to stop working so hard."

"And now there are those tips they're getting at the police department, too," I said. "What do you suppose those are about?"

Mom mumbled in her sleep. It was hard to understand the words—something with a lot of os. Then her eyes blinked open. "Wha...oh, hi. I wasn't talking in my sleep again, was I?"

The next day was Sunday. When I got downstairs, Dad was sitting at the dining room table with our newspaper, the *Middle Daily Times*.

"Take a look at this!" He held up the front page, and I saw that my friend Tim Roberts—he's a reporter—had succeeded where Sophie and I had failed.

Green Power Revolution Imminent, Scientist Claims

New Professor Calls 'Grassoline' A Game Changer

College Expects Billions, Critics Call Idea Overhyped

By Tim Roberts

College Springs— *"Grassoline," brainchild of the college's newest faculty member, Tom Henry, is the fuel of the future—an inexpensive, green power source for motor vehicles and electric generators, proponents say. Once in mass production, the clean-burning biofuel is expected to replace traditional fossil fuels like oil, coal, and natural gas.*

Furthermore, grassoline has the potential to boost the regional economy while also yielding big profits for the college, Henry himself, and investors.

Professor Tom Henry left a well-known California university to take his current post. To lure him to Pennsylvania, college officials reportedly offered him a pay package worthy of a football coach, a well-equipped and spacious laboratory complex, and an abundance of graduate students and researchers.

Interviewed this week at the lab—located on the

north side of campus beyond the stadium—Henry said his new biofuel is game-changing technology.

"Making fuel out of lawn clippings eliminates the environmental damage done by extracting oil, coal, or gas," Henry said. "Likewise, the supply of fossil fuels is limited, whereas grassoline is always renewable. Grassoline also burns clean, limiting carbon emissions and associated atmospheric harm.

"Obviously," Henry concluded, "the benefits of my research for mankind and the earth will be enormous."

To make grassoline, Henry and his team use a combination of chemicals to break down the cell structure of lawn clippings. The resulting slurry is then heated and steam condensed into a flammable liquid, grassoline.

Henry acknowledged that challenges remain. At present, for example, it takes more energy to produce grassoline than the grassoline itself delivers.

The missing ingredient? An inexpensive agent for catalyzing cellular breakdown.

Asked about the difficulty of finding such an agent, Henry refused to go into specifics, saying only, "We daily expect the breakthrough we need."

And such a breakthrough can't come too quickly. Competing teams at other universities are working on similar projects. The team that gets its biofuel to the marketplace first is the team that will reap the rewards.

While many college officials applaud Henry and his work, the professor does have his critics. Among them is Enzo Olivo, director of the college's fossil fuels institute. Olivo believes that any effective catalyzing agent for the manufacturing process would also be impractical.

"The only chemical agents with the potential to serve my esteemed colleague's purposes are extremely volatile," Olivo said. "While the dream of an economical, renewable energy is dear to us all, grassoline is only pie in the sky."

"Pie in the sky?" I said when I finished reading. "What's that?"

Dad grinned. "A great name for my new business—what do you think?"

"It's better than Parakeet Pies," I said. "But what does this Enzo Olivo guy mean? Oh—wasn't he the one with the beard at the party last night?"

Dad nodded. "He was there—arguing with Professor Henry. And what *pie in the sky* means is 'too good to be true.'"

I looked at the story again, then asked Dad for help understanding the tricky parts. In the end, I got the basic idea: Professor Henry was working on a way to manufacture gas out of lawn clippings. It would be good for the environment and also make lots of people rich, including Professor Henry. But there was one ingredient still missing in the man-ufacturing process, and he and his team had to hurry up and find it.

"I only have one more question," I said. "What's *volatile?*"

"Might blow up," Dad said.

"Yikes!" I said. "I hope the Henrys didn't bring anything *volatile* with them from California."

CHAPTER FOUR

After breakfast, I did my chores—washed dishes, swept the kitchen floor, and took out the trash. Then I played video games till it was time for my friend Russell's birthday party, which was at his house this year. I had wanted to get him a gift card, but Mom said that was impersonal, so I got him a mini-football instead.

Everyone else got him a gift card.

Russell only lives a couple of blocks from my house, so I walked there. On the way home, I noticed that someone had shoveled the snow in front of the house that's under construction on Groundhog Boulevard. Even though it was started like two years ago, there are only walls, and a roof made out of blue plastic—no doors or windows. Dad says the people who were building it ran out of money. Sometimes teenagers sneak in, and Mom or Officer Krichels has to go scare them away.

I had only been home long enough to take off my gloves, coat, and boots when the doorbell rang. It was Eve, and she had Marshmallow behind her on a leash. In her hand was a white envelope with my name on it.

"Is it a party invitation? Cool! Hey, come in if you want."

I opened the card, which was black and silver and gold. On the front was a picture of a cake and a glass of fizzy punch. It looked very grown-up, just like the date, December 31, New Year's Eve.

I had never gotten a party invitation for New Year's Eve before. I was psyched!

We were still in the hall when Luau appeared, saw Eve's dog, and immediately did his best imitation of a haunted-house cat—arched his back, showed his teeth, and said *Ssssssst*. Then he went back to normal, looked at me and blinked, meaning, *Scary, huh?*

"Ease up on him, wouldja?" I said to Luau.

Meanwhile, Marshmallow was behind Eve's snow boots, whining, *Help—big orange dude gonna get me!*

"No, he won't," I reassured the dog. "His hiss is worse than his bite."

Eve looked at Luau, then Marshmallow, then me. "You talk to dogs, too?"

Wait—did I? Till then I had only talked to Luau, and that was because the two of us grew up together. We were even born the same day. But thinking about it, I remembered I had understood Marshmallow at the Henrys' house the day before—when he said, *How can something be bad if it tastes good?*

I didn't want to lie to Eve. But I didn't want to tell the whole truth either. I mean, if you met some person who claimed he talked to animals—and his name wasn't Dr. Dolittle—wouldn't you be a little freaked out?

So what I said was "Seriously?" which didn't mean anything. Then I changed the subject. "Who else are you inviting?"

"Pretty much everybody older than fifth grade," Eve said. "But I guess Yasmeen isn't allowed to go. Probably she wouldn't want to, anyway, after I laughed at her last night. I feel really bad about it."

"Did you take her an invitation?" I asked.

Eve nodded. "I dropped one off. Her little brother took it. What's his name? Jeremiah? Anyway, nobody in that family likes me. He never even smiled."

"That doesn't mean anything with Jeremiah," I said. "It's just how his face works. Jeremiah worries all the time."

"Whatever." Eve sighed. "But I feel like where we lived in California, everybody liked my family. And here already people hate us. That article in the paper today didn't help. It made us sound rich and snooty—my dad, at least."

"I know you're not!" I said. "I know you're normal."

"Yeah?" Eve looked hopeful. "And that Sophie girl, she's a little different, but she seems friendly."

I nodded. "Yeah, different and friendly pretty much sums up Sophie. Anyway, your party will give you a chance to show everybody how nice and normal you are, right? Trust me. Things are gonna work out fine."

CHAPTER FIVE

Before we got out for break, my English teacher, Ms. Caylor, had assigned us to write a holiday journal, with at least one complete sentence every day. Ms. Caylor is old and thinks kids these days are pretty dumb. She said she was giving us the journal assignment so we wouldn't "lose whatever meager reading and writing skills had been gained during first semester."

I decided I'd show *her* by writing at least *two* sentences every day—and maybe even more.

Here's my journal up till December 29, the day before life on Chickadee Court went totally crazy:

Saturday, Dec. 17: *Today I took a pie to our new neighbors' house. The pie fell on the floor. It wasn't my fault. Also, there was the regular holiday party at the Jensens' house. It was a disaster.*

Sunday, Dec. 18: *Today I went to Russell's birthday party. Next year I am giving him a gift card.*

Monday, Dec. 19: *I helped my dad pack pies in boxes and washed dishes. I needed to earn money for Christmas shopping.*

Tuesday, Dec. 20: *I went Christmas shopping with Dad. For a police officer, my mom is kind of girly. I bought her smelly hand lotion. I bought my cat a mouse stuffed with catnip. I don't mean a real mouse. The mouse was made out of cloth.*

Wednesday, Dec. 21: *I went Christmas shopping with Mom. I bought Dad a murder mystery book with a picture of blood on the cover. I picked it so he could think about something besides pies.*

Thursday, Dec. 22: *I visited my friend Bub. He made Italian soup with vegetables and noodles. I ate two bowls. The name of this soup starts with M, but I don't know how to spell it.*

Friday, Dec. 23: *It snowed. I hung out with Yasmeen. She is my best friend who happens to be a girl. Later I went to Eve's house. Eve is a new girl on my street. I told her I would come to her birthday party. Her birthday party is on New*

Year's Eve. Get it? Yasmeen does not like Eve. It is too complicated to explain why.

Saturday, Dec. 24: *My family and Yasmeen's family ate a fish dinner at Bub's house with his niece, Jo. We did that last year for Christmas Eve, too. We sang Christmas carols after we ate. Yasmeen has been taking singing lessons. Her voice is loud.*

Sunday, Dec. 25: *It snowed more. Santa brought me Lousy Luigi 4. Santa also brought books and clothes. (At my house, Santa is really my parents.) A surprise was I got a light-up Frisbee from Sophie Sikora. She also gave Frisbees to the other kids on our street. It was generous. It was also showing off. Sophie likes to brag about how her family has so much money.*

Santa gave Yasmeen a purple coat.

My parents liked their presents. Luau liked his mouse.

Monday, Dec. 26: *Bub, Yasmeen, and I delivered Dad's pies. Then we watched Christmas movies. Bub always tells about the actor in* It's a Wonderful Life. *His name is Jimmy Stewart. He grew up in Pennsylvania.*

I know, Bub!

Tuesday, Dec. 27: *I got up late. I played Johnny Annoy Football and Lousy Luigi 4. We ate hamburgers for dinner. It was a perfect day.*

Wednesday, Dec. 28: *Please see Tuesday. (I hope that is a complete sentence.) The other thing that happened is Eve came over. She said she is getting a surprise for her birthday. Her parents told her it is something big. She also said most kids are coming to her party. However, Yasmeen is not coming. I felt bad when Eve said that. I wish she and Yasmeen could be friends.*

Thursday, Dec. 29: *Today it was 50 degrees. Mom says the people in charge of Ice Carnival are worried. They think the ice sculptures might melt.*

CHAPTER SIX

On Friday morning, the last Friday of the holiday break, a barking dog woke me.

It was Marshmallow. He was inside his house. But even from far away I knew what he was saying: *Danger! Danger! Danger!*

I guess I didn't need mad skills to translate that.

Before I could roll over and look out the window, Luau jumped on my chest, circled around, and head-butted my face: *Would somebody hit the mute button on that dog?*

"Good morning to you, too, buddy," I said. "What's going on at the Henrys' house, anyway?"

I pushed the curtain aside and saw that it was going to be another sunny day. In the Henrys' driveway was a yellow Al's Delivery Service van. Marshmallow was barking because Al and another man were unloading something big that was wrapped in white cloth. On top of it was an extra-large orange bow.

This must be Eve's surprise present! They had it on a hand truck, one of those wheelie things some people call a dolly. Slowly and with a lot of noise, the guys wheeled it across the Henrys' yard and positioned it beside the five gold rings.

My clock said 9:07. Back before Pie in the Sky, Dad would never have let me sleep in this late; he would have come bounding up the stairs to wake me with some stupid joke at eight.

Now I was a victim of parental neglect.

On the other hand, a little neglect isn't so bad if it means you get to sleep in.

I shoved the covers to the floor, threw on jeans and a T-shirt, and ran downstairs. There was no time for brushing my teeth or washing my face.

"Oh, arisen from the dead, have we?" Dad was sitting on a stool studying a cookbook.

"Come on!" I said. "Something's going on at the Henrys' house."

Dad looked at the timer on the oven. "Okay. I've got a few minutes."

By the time we got outside, a knot of neighbors—mostly kids—had gathered on the sidewalk. Jeremiah Popp was there, along with Billy Jensen. So were Sophie and Byron Sikora. I asked Jeremiah about Yasmeen. He shook his head and frowned. "She said it's too cold to come outside and I should just tell her what the fuss is about."

Dad looked down at Jeremiah. "It's not that

cold, and besides, Yasmeen is usually tougher than any kid of mine."

"Meaning me?" I asked.

"If the coat fits," Dad said. "Now, what is under that tarpaulin, do you think?"

Tarpaulin? Isn't that some kind of big turtle?

Usually Yasmeen would define it for me. But Jeremiah stepped up. "A tarpaulin is a tarp, Alex. He's talking about that white cloth there."

"I knew that," I said. "But I don't know what's under it. Sophie, ask your uncle, why don't you?" Al the delivery guy is Sophie's mom's brother.

But Sophie's uncle wouldn't tell us. "What's it look like?" he teased.

Billy Jensen guessed baby tree, and Jeremiah said humongous bird feeder. All I could think of was a soda machine.

Finally Eve came out the front door, carrying Marshmallow. Her mom and dad brought up the rear. Eve was grinning as she ran across the yard and spoke to the other guy, the one I didn't know. He had a beard. "Uncle Jim," she said, "what are you doing here? What is this thing? Is it for me?"

Not for nothing do I have a reputation for being a detective. If this guy was Eve's uncle, then I had an idea what the surprise might be. Hadn't Eve's mom said he was a sculptor?

"Pull the tarp off and see for yourself!" Eve's uncle handed her a corner of the cloth, and Eve wasted no time—she yanked.

Sure enough, the tarp dropped to reveal a sculpture—an ice sculpture!

But that wasn't all.

Glittering before us in the sunshine, the present was a life-sized ice replica of Eve herself. Same height. Same hair. Same big smile. She was wearing shorts and skater shoes and a tank top, standing on a skateboard, arms out for balance and hair flying. The board was tilted with her on it, so that she seemed to be screaming down a hill.

There was an instant of silence while everyone stared. Then Dad breathed, "Oh. My. Goodness."

And I said, "Wow—that is so cool!"

And Dad punched me in the arm for making a dumb joke, but really I didn't even mean it as a joke.

Then everybody spoke at the same time, and the No. 1 reaction was: "Amazing!"

The real Eve, the flesh-and-blood one, loved it so much she squealed—which scared Marshmallow, who jumped out of her arms, sat back on his haunches, and barked at Ice Eve. *I don't like this. I don't like this one bit. She doesn't smell right.* Then, like he wanted to commit the scent to memory, he trotted to the base of the sculpture and sniffed it all around.

"You don't suppose the pooch will, uh…try to mark his territory?" Dad asked.

"Ewww!" I said.

But Marshmallow behaved himself. Meanwhile, Uncle Jim told Eve the present had been her dad's idea. "So if you don't like it, blame him. And if you do, I get the credit. A good likeness, huh?"

"Scary good," Eve said, and to me that seemed about right.

The thing is, the sculpture really did look like Eve—a cold, lifeless version of Eve, with a frozen stare and a frozen smile. Yeah, it was awesome. But it was also *creepy!*

I'm not sure everybody else felt the same, though. They all wanted a picture of Eve in front of the statue, and she didn't mind posing. She even stood the way the statue was standing, arms out and head tilted back. There was lots of chatting and laughing, and Eve's parents looked proud. They had done a good job with their birthday surprise.

And there was something else good, too. It was nice to see the neighbors getting along. It looked as if the Jensens' disaster party had been forgotten. Now I wished maybe Professor and Mrs. Popp would come outside—even Yasmeen. Maybe they could start over and be friends.

But so far there was no sign of them.

Finally, Eve's uncle Jim said he had to get going. He had a lot more sculptures to set up downtown. "It's my busiest day of the year," he said.

Dad and I helped him fold the tarp; then he put it under his arm and started toward the van. On his way, he took one look back. In the warm sun, a stray drop like a tear slid down Ice Eve's cheek. Uncle Jim frowned and looked at the blue sky. "It's not supposed to be this warm in December!"

CHAPTER SEVEN

Yasmeen phoned after breakfast. She wanted to know what I was doing with my day.

Yasmeen believes in doing something with your day. This is a basic difference between her and me.

"I have to go get Eve a birthday present," I said. "Are you sure your parents won't let you go to her party? You can sleep in the next morning."

"No, I can't. I have church," Yasmeen said.

"You can take a nap after church," I said. "My mom's day off is tomorrow. She'll talk to your mom if it will help."

"I don't even want to go to her old party," Yasmeen said. "But I'll come with you to get a present. I mean, I'm busy but not that busy."

Dad had to make pie deliveries later that morning, so he dropped Yasmeen and me off downtown. We bought cups of hot spiced cider from a booth at the Ice Carnival, then walked around to look at the sculptures.

Yasmeen liked the one by the flower shop, a girl holding a bouquet. My favorite was the one in front of the pet store, a dog sitting on its haunches and begging. Eve's uncle had made the sculpture so detailed you could see the curls in the dog's fur. There were lots of others, too—like an ice football player in front of a store that sells college souvenirs and T-shirts, a chef with a tray of pizza in front of a restaurant, and—this one was boring—a dollar sign in front of a bank.

Finally, we came to Mrs. Miggins's toy store, where I was planning to get the present.

"How come Mrs. Miggins doesn't have a sculpture outside?" Yasmeen wanted to know.

"Because she doesn't like Ice Carnival," I explained. "She says there's no point having an event after Christmas because nobody buys toys after Christmas. She wants the city to move the carnival earlier, but they won't."

Inside, we were greeted by Mrs. Miggins's Saint Bernard, Leo G.

"Hey, buddy," I said. Then—before I could get out of the way—he shook his hairy head and let fly with a wad of dog drool.

"*Yeccch.*" Yasmeen stared at the mess on my sleeve. "Alex, I think you attract that stuff."

Mrs. Miggins brought me a paper towel. While I did my best to clean up, she asked if she could help us find anything.

I started to say yes. What do I know about a girl's birthday present?

But Yasmeen spoke first. "We've got it under control."

Then, with Mrs. Miggins watching in case we broke anything, we walked around the store. I picked up a game, a stuffed animal, and a puzzle, but Yasmeen's opinion on all of them was "Too expensive—you hardly know her!"

This was not helpful.

Finally we came to the bargain table. On it was a jack-o'-lantern key chain left over from Halloween. It made a scream noise when you squeezed it.

Yasmeen picked it up. "Perfect!"

"Are you kidding? It would give a person nightmares!"

"But look, Alex," Yasmeen said, "it's marked down seventy-five percent. Trust me, Eve will love it."

I lost my temper. "Yasmeen, what is the matter with you? I can get Eve a decent present if I want to!"

Yasmeen's face went through a bunch of changes—she was surprised, she was mad, she was sad—she was *really* mad.

And then…she turned and walked out of the store!

What the heck?

"Wait—come back!" I called, but the door was swinging shut.

My face felt hot, and the rest of me felt terrible. Leo G. came up and bumped my behind in sympathy—leaving a spot of drool on my jeans.

Mrs. Miggins had been watching. "Everything okay there, Alex? Now can I help you out?"

"Oh, uh...sure," I said, and explained what I was shopping for.

Mrs. Miggins was less grumpy than usual, probably because the store was almost empty, minimizing the chance that something might get broken. "Ah, I see," she said. "You know, the Henry girl and her mom came in to shop for party favors. Very nice people. Yasmeen might be afraid she'll lose you."

"Lose me?" I repeated. "I'm not going anywhere."

It wasn't a joke, but Mrs. Miggins laughed. Then she had a good idea for a present. "How about one of these light-up Frisbees? Like the ones Sophie Sikora got you and the other kids for Christmas? I'll even wrap it in birthday paper for you."

Dad picked me up on his way home from delivering pies.

"What happened to Yasmeen?" he asked after I

tossed the present in the car and climbed in beside him.

I had just started to explain when we spotted someone wearing a purple coat on the sidewalk ahead—Yasmeen. Dad pulled the car over and rolled down the passenger window. "Hey, Ms. Popp," he said. "May I offer you a lift?"

Yasmeen looked across me at my dad. "That's okay, Mr. Parakeet. I prefer to walk. Thank you very much, though."

Dad tried to argue, but Yasmeen wouldn't budge.

"Okay." He shrugged. "Walk safely, then." We both waved, and he drove away.

"When we get home, I'll call her parents so they know what's up," he said. "Boy, she must be mad. What did you do?"

"*Nothing!* And thanks for thinking it's my fault." The rest of the way home I finished explaining what had happened. In our driveway I added the crazy thing Mrs. Miggins had said about how Yasmeen might be worried she'd lose me.

"I don't get it," I concluded.

Dad turned the ignition switch to off, sat for a second, and then looked over like he wanted to say something.

I didn't give him a chance. "You're not going to get all wise and parental on me, are you?"

Dad smiled. "Parental maybe, but I don't have a lot of wisdom to offer. Girls are tricky, Alex, and—"

"*Girls!?*" I couldn't believe my dad. "Who said this had anything to do with *girls?*"

"Uh, Earth to Alex? Yasmeen and Eve are girls."

"Only technically," I said.

Dad grinned. "Okay, have it your way. Hey—isn't there a bowl game we could watch this afternoon? I think I could use a break from making pies."

Yasmeen didn't call the rest of that day. I wasn't used to having her mad at me, and when I went to bed I couldn't sleep. Finally, I raised myself up on my elbows and looked out the window. In the Henrys' yard, I could see Ice Eve in front of the five gold rings. Sparkling in the colored lights, she didn't look creepy or zombie-like anymore. She looked pretty.

Was Dad right? Did this thing with Yasmeen and Eve and me have something to do with them being *girls?* It was all very confusing.

CHAPTER EIGHT

Mom opened my door the next morning before it was even light out. "Alex? Get up, honey. I need you. Something's happened at the Henrys.'"

I rubbed my eyes and sat up, disturbing Luau, who jumped from bed to floor—*buh-bump*—then swished his tail and blinked: *Well! And I was having such a lovely dream about herring.*

"I know it's early." This was Mom's idea of an apology. "And I'll meet you downstairs in five."

Mom closed the door. I counted to three, swung my feet to the floor, stood up, put clothes on, splashed water on my face, and went downstairs— all without waking up.

In the front hall, Mom looked at her watch and nodded. "Impressive. But you might do something to your hair. You wouldn't want to scare anybody, would you?"

"What's going on?" I flattened my hair with one hand and grabbed my coat with the other. "It's your day off, I thought."

Mom pushed the front door open. "Eve's gone."

"*What?!*" I hurried out behind her and the cold air woke me at last. The sky was dark and cloudy, with a pale gray light at the horizon.

"*Ice* Eve, I mean," Mom clarified. "'Though when you think about it, that's even more mysterious. Eve the girl has working legs, while Eve the statue doesn't."

By now we were passing the Lees' geese a-laying, all present and accounted for. Next door in the Henrys' yard, the rings were fine, too. But Mom was right. Ice Eve was gone.

"Isn't it possible she disappeared into a puddle?" I asked.

Mom shook her head. "It takes days to melt a big chunk of ice like that, even in summer."

Our arrival on the Henrys' walk caused a yappy outburst from Marshmallow, who was peeking out the front window over the back of the sofa: *Danger! Danger! Danger!*

Honestly, did that dog have bad eyesight or a bad memory?

Mrs. Henry—Jessica—opened the door for Mom and me. Marshmallow had jumped off the sofa by now and was running zigzags in the front hall. When we walked in, he hid behind Mrs. Henry's feet and quivered.

"Thanks for coming over," Mrs. Henry said to

Mom. "Would you like a cup of coffee? Eve's in the dining room, Alex."

The moms disappeared into the kitchen. I went to find Eve. She was sitting at the head of the table. She was still wearing pajamas, the lucky pup. Her chin was resting on her hand. It was the first time I'd ever seen her look sad.

"Hey." I sat down. "What happened?"

Eve looked at me and made a face. I think it was supposed to be a smile, but it didn't work out so well.

"You don't have to tell me if you don't want to," I said quickly.

"There's nothing to tell," Eve said. "Somebody stole me—stole Ice Eve, I mean."

I don't know if I've mentioned this yet, but Yasmeen and I—with help from Sophie and Luau and some other people—have solved four mysteries on our street. Not to brag, but we are actually kind of good at the whole detecting thing.

So now, even though I felt bad for Eve, my professional skills kicked in. A case to solve meant questions to ask.

"When did you notice Ice Eve was missing?" I said.

Eve looked at me. "Oh, wow, is this like you're being a detective all of a sudden?"

"That's my mom's job," I said modestly. "But sometimes I do help her out."

"Yeah, I heard," Eve said. "There were stories in the newspaper, right? I even hoped maybe someday I'd get to help you and Yasmeen solve a case. But I never wanted it to be my *own* case. Alex—I *hate* living here. The weather's cold. No one likes me. And now somebody stole my birthday present."

CHAPTER NINE

This was awful. There were tears in Eve's eyes. Wasn't this a girl kind of conversation? Where was Yasmeen when I needed her?

Home in bed, probably. Even Yasmeen didn't get up this early on vacation.

"Uh…*I* like you," I said, because I had to say something. "I mean, I don't mean *like* like you, not the way some people mean *like*—some *girls* mean *like*, I mean—but just *like* like. Like not dislike. Does that make sense?"

Now Eve actually did smile. "Yeah, it does. Thanks. And I like you, too. Meaning *like* the same way you mean *like*, I think."

Now we were done with the awful part, right? So I tried again. "When did you notice Ice Eve was missing?"

Eve thought for a second. "I got up early 'cause I knew Mom was making carrot muffins for breakfast, and I looked out the window, and I saw the five gold rings but not the statue. And the weird thing is I didn't even think about it then. I guess you don't necessarily notice when something is gone, the way you notice when something is there. Does that make sense?"

"If you say so," I said.

"It wasn't till I got downstairs that my brain said *wait a sec,* and I opened the front door and looked out. That's when I *really* saw that Ice Eve was missing. It was still dark, but she was definitely gone."

"And what time was that?" I asked.

"Maybe an hour ago," Eve said.

I looked at my watch. It was only 7:45—so she was talking 6:45.

"And when did you last see the statue?" I asked.

Eve had to think before she spoke. "When I went to bed last night. I looked out my window. The Christmas lights were still on and the music was playing—so it must have been before eleven, when Professor Jensen turns all that off. Maybe ten o'clock?"

I remembered seeing the statue last night, too—probably around the same time.

"So the statue disappeared between ten last night and six-forty-five this morning," I said. "But probably after eleven, because whoever took it would've waited till the lights were off. Did you hear anything unusual during that time?"

Eve shook her head. "I slept great."

The door from the kitchen opened, and Mrs. Henry brought out a plate with four muffins on it. I did some quick calculations. If Eve had already had one, or if she was too upset to eat, I could score as many as three.

And I am a growing boy.

We didn't talk about the case while we ate. Instead, Eve told me about her school in California, where the kids wear flip-flops and cut-off pajama bottoms all year long, and even some white kids have dreadlocks. It was obvious Eve thought California was pretty great.

The only bad part was her dad had had to work all the time. She had hoped maybe that would change when they moved to Pennsylvania, but so far it hadn't. Some nights—like last night—he worked all night in his new lab.

Mrs. Henry came out of the kitchen and took the muffin plate. My mom was behind her.

"What do you say we go outside and look for some physical evidence?" Mom said. "I'm betting our thief left tracks."

Fortified by muffins—I only got two; Eve turned out to have a healthy appetite—we put coats on and went outside. Marshmallow came, too. It was light by now, and the clouds had cleared away. On the spot where Ice Eve had stood on her skateboard yesterday was a patch of snow packed into a neat square of ice. Same as he had with the statue, Marshmallow sniffed around it and whined. *Still doesn't smell right. I don't like it.*

There weren't any footprints, probably because the snow was too icy and hard to take them. But we did follow two shallow parallel grooves from the neat square to the sidewalk. Next to the curb, the grooves became a confused jumble of frozen mud.

"Someone put Ice Eve on a hand truck, it looks like," Mom said, "and then hauled her across the yard and manhandled her into a waiting truck." There was no snow on the street, so we couldn't see tire tracks. Mom said, "I can have Officer Krichels come out with one of the lab guys to check for residue from the vehicle tires. That might tell us more."

Mrs. Henry looked surprised. "You want to call forensics? Isn't this just a prank?"

Mom shrugged. "The ice sculpture was worth enough money that stealing it counts as a felony. But if you don't want to follow up, the district attorney probably won't, either. The theft of a single ice sculpture is upsetting, but it doesn't threaten the public."

"It's your present that was stolen, Eve," Mrs. Henry said. "What do you think?"

Eve shook her head. "I don't want to make a

big deal out of it. By the time we find it, it'll be a bucket of water. On the other hand"—she looked at me—"maybe Alex and I could do some detecting. I mean, if you're not busy, Alex? I never did detecting before."

I was surprised to realize I liked this idea. Detecting is a lot of work, but vacation had gone on long enough that I was actually bored.

"Okay," I said, but then I had a horrible thought. Yasmeen would kill me if Eve and I worked together, unless...maybe the three of us could do it? Maybe if they worked together, Eve and Yasmeen would get to be friends.

It was still early, and Eve still had to get dressed. We decided to meet at my house in an hour to make a plan. Meanwhile, I had a plan of my own— and two minutes later, I was standing on the Popps' front porch.

I put my finger on the doorbell and paused. Yasmeen couldn't possibly be mad at me anymore, right? Plus, she loves detecting. When she found out Ice Eve was missing, she'd totally want to investigate.

I took a breath and pressed the bell. Right away, like she'd been waiting on the other side, Yasmeen opened the door.

CHAPTER TEN

"Hi, bud!" I smiled. "How ya doin'?"

Yasmeen didn't smile back. Instead, she tilted her head to one side, folded her arms across her chest, and said, "Yes?"

I kept smiling. "So—I guess you're still mad, right?"

Yasmeen narrowed her eyes. "What do you think?"

"Well...okay, anyway, that's too bad because..." and I explained about Ice Eve.

Yasmeen listened closely, then stepped over the threshold so she could look down the street at the Henrys' yard. Was I imagining it, or did a smile flicker on her face when she saw that Ice Eve was gone?

Something crazy crossed my mind. Could Yasmeen have had anything to do with it? Solving mysteries had taught both of us how bad guys operate. If Yasmeen wanted to steal something, she totally knew how.

The human brain is a wonderful thing, because somehow I managed to think these thoughts and talk at the same time. Finally I got to the point: "So, Yasmeen, could you help us, please? Except for my mom, you're the best detective on Chickadee Court."

It was pretty obvious I was buttering her up, but sometimes she falls for it.

"Who is 'us'?" she said.

"Eve and me," I said, and right away I knew I'd made a mistake.

"No," she said. "I'm busy. Goodbye, Alex."

She started to close the door, but I stuck my foot between it and the jamb. That's an old detecting trick. "What are you so busy with?"

"Practicing for choir auditions," Yasmeen said. Then she startled me by opening her mouth and singing: *"Uh-MAY-zi-i-ing grace, how-ow sweeeeet the sound..."*

I gritted my teeth but resisted the urge to cover my ears. From somewhere in the house, Jeremiah called, "Yasmeen, you promised! Enough with the la-la-la!"

Yasmeen closed her mouth and frowned.

"That was great!" I lied. "You're definitely improving. Eve won't mind if you want to practice while we investigate. It'll be like a whole new thing—the singing detective. What do you think?"

"I think not," Yasmeen said. "Besides, I'm not sure there really *is* a mystery. Eve probably hid the statue herself—or perhaps she poured boiling water on top to melt it."

"Why would she do that?"

"To get attention," Yasmeen said. "She's that kind of girl. She planned her own birthday party, didn't she?"

"With her *mom*," I said, "and anyway, she had to. She doesn't know anybody here yet."

Yasmeen sighed. "I should have known you'd defend her. Now, if you'll excuse me, I'm reading a really great book—*The Hound of the Baskervilles*. Ever hear of it?"

I shook my head.

"It's a Sherlock Holmes book," she said, "and I'm just at the part where I find out who did it. Bye, Alex." And this time she succeeded in closing the door.

I was on the sidewalk walking home when I saw Mom pulling the car out of our driveway. "Hey!" I motioned for her to roll down the window. "It's your day off! You're not going to work, are you?"

"Kind of an emergency," she said. "Call you later—I might need your help. Love you, honey."

And she drove away.

"Dad?" I called when I got inside. "What's Mom's big emergency, anyway?"

There was no answer, and I remembered it was Saturday, which meant Dad was probably grocery shopping. I hung up my coat and sat down on the floor to un-Velcro my boots. Meanwhile, Luau padded in from the den, head-butted my arm, and purred to tell me how very much he'd missed me.

"Unh-hunh." I kicked my boots off and scratched behind his ears. "What is it you really want?"

Luau sat back, raised his paw to do a quick face wash, and then looked me in the eye. *In your defense, it* was *a busy morning.*

Oh, shoot. "Sorry, buddy. Come on."

I got to my feet and headed for the basement, where I poured Luau a bowl of breakfast. Luau didn't stop to *mrrf* a thank-you, but when he took his first bite, he purred, which was good enough. Then I remembered I hadn't eaten breakfast yet myself—unless you count a couple of carrot muffins. And I hadn't brushed my teeth or washed my face or made my bed, either.

I went upstairs, cleaned up, and was just tugging my bedspread flat when the doorbell rang. Had it been an hour already? I hoped the day would settle down soon. I didn't think I could continue to live at this pace.

Eve was wearing orange pants and a pale-green turtleneck and a pink jacket. There were stars on the pink jacket. Her snow boots were purple, and her ear warmers matched her snow boots. Most of my friends have dark winter coats and black snow boots, so Eve looked kind of eye-popping.

"I'm ready for detecting! And I've got this idea, too—if it's okay with you, that is."

If it's okay with you, that is? Did she really say that? Already, I could tell detecting with Eve was going to be different than detecting with Yasmeen.

"I'm sure your idea is great," I said. "Come on in for a sec while I put on my coat. Then we can go."

"Where are we going?" Eve asked.

"Bub's," I said.

Eve's eyes got big. "You mean Bub's a suspect? Do we get to interrogate him?"

"Not exactly," I said. "We're going to Bub's because minestrone soup makes a tasty and nutritious breakfast. Also, he's the best one to give you your first lesson in detecting."

CHAPTER ELEVEN

Bub lives on the corner of Chickadee and Ground-hog, and it's not only *people* who like to hang out with him. Luau does, too. Done with breakfast, my cat followed Eve and me down the sidewalk with his orange tail flying like a flag.

As we walked, Eve explained her idea. She had made a LOST ICE SCULPTURE flyer on her computer, and she thought we should post it all over the neighborhood.

"Only, our printer's not hooked up yet," she said. "So I can't make copies."

"We could use our printer, but it's slow," I said. "How about if we ask Sophie to print them out? Only, if we do, she's going to want to help us with detecting."

"That's okay with me," Eve said.

We passed the Ryans' house—partridge in a pear tree—then turned into Bub's driveway, where a yellow Al's Delivery Service van was already parked.

"Come on in!" Bub called when he heard us on the steps. "Soup's on, and the coffee's hot!"

When you walk into Bub's house, the hallway's in front, and the living room's on the right. Inside the living room are a recliner and a sofa, besides a dining table with six chairs around it. Beyond that is the kitchen, where the soup is. The drill is Bub makes soup every morning; then anyone who stops by can serve himself or herself from the pot on the stove.

Luau immediately jumped into his usual spot on the recliner, circled twice, and made himself comfortable. The recliner faces the TV, which was on with the sound on mute. Luau likes old black-and-white movies, especially ones with cat food commercials. The one on the TV now had cowboys.

Bub was sitting at the head of the table, with Al and a surprise guest—Sophie Sikora herself. In front of her on the table was a plastic box and a bunch of teensy parts and pieces. I had to look twice to realize they used to be a calculator; the box was so big and clunky looking, it must have dated from Jurassic times.

Did I mention Sophie is some kind of an electronics genius? She can fix anything—doorbells, baby monitors, remote controls. Sometimes this comes in handy when we're detecting.

Everybody said hi, and Bub offered us minestrone.

Of course I said "totally" to the soup, but first I explained how Ice Eve was missing.

"Your birthday present?" Al looked at Eve. "That's a shame. Hard to imagine going to the trouble of stealing it. She was one heavy girl."

I looked at Bub and Sophie. "You didn't hear anything last night, did you? We figure she must've disappeared between eleven and about six in the morning."

Bub thought he'd heard a car sometime in the night, but he hadn't looked at the clock. Sophie hadn't heard anything. "But I'm a sound sleeper," she added.

"So you're detecting again, are you?" Bub asked me. "Where's Yasmeen?"

"You mean you don't think I can solve a case without Yasmeen?" I said.

"I didn't say that," Bub said, "but up till now, you and Yasmeen have been a team."

Sophie cleared her throat—*"Ahem"*—and wagged her thumbs at herself.

"You and Yasmeen *and* Sophie," Bub said quickly.

"Will you help us, Sophie?" Eve asked. "And it would be great if Yasmeen wanted to help, too."

Before the whole thing about Yasmeen could get awkward, I changed the subject—told Sophie about the flyer and asked if her family's printer might be available.

"*No problemo,*" Sophie said. "And I bet Byron and his buddies would be happy to put them up, too. With school out, they're driving Mom crazy, and she can tell them they're helping with a mystery. Can you e-mail me the file, Eve?"

Eve said her mom would do it, and they each got out their phones.

I don't have a phone.

And I don't have a parent available to serve as my personal assistant. Yasmeen doesn't have those things, either. Maybe that's one reason she and I have always gotten along?

Always till now, I mean.

While the girls arranged things about the flyers, I went into the kitchen and served Eve and myself bowls of soup. When we were all settled back at the dining room table, I asked Bub to explain to Eve about solving a crime.

"Shucks." Bub tried to look modest. "You mean you want me to serve in the way of an expert consultant?"

I nodded. "If you hadn't shared all you know about mysteries from watching detective movies, Yasmeen and I never would have solved a single mystery."

Bub leaned back in his chair and twiddled his thumbs, which he always does when he's thinking. "Well, Eve, I can break it down for you right quick. How you solve a mystery is, you look for the culprit who has three things: means, motive, and opportunity. *Means* means a way to do it. Now, in this case, that's what you'd call critical, because not so many people have a way to steal an ice sculpture."

I slurped a bit of soup and nodded. "Good point."

"So in this case, I'd say you're looking for someone with a truck, for example. And a dolly. And plenty of upper-body strength."

Bub looked pointedly at Al, who made a body-builder pose to show his biceps. "I've got all of the above," he said, "but I didn't do it."

"Okay, means makes sense," Eve said. "What about motive?"

"Motive," Bub said, "means you're looking for the culprit who some way or another benefits from the crime."

"Yeah—and who would benefit from owning a big lump of ice?" I asked.

Eve looked at me. "Hey!"

"Oh, sorry," I said. "A big lump of…uh…very cute ice?"

"That's better," Eve said.

"Maybe the thief didn't want the ice," Sophie said. "Maybe the thief just didn't want Eve to have a nice birthday."

"But nobody here even knows me!" Eve said.

Sophie said some people are just mean and started to tell a long story about her little brother, Byron. Sophie talks a lot, and sometimes she gets way, way off the subject. I held up my hand. "Sophie? We want to solve this case before the spring thaw. So can we make a deal? If you're talking too much, I make a sign so you know to be quiet."

"What sign?" Sophie asked.

"You could tug on your earlobe," Al said.

"Which earlobe?" Sophie wanted to know.

"Either earlobe!" I said—because I was afraid I'd forget and tug the wrong one and Sophie would just keep talking.

"But what if you have an itchy earlobe?" Sophie asked.

I looked at her.

"*Fine!*" Sophie said. "How about if I just don't say anything at all for the rest of the investigation? Would *that* make you happy?"

From his chair, Luau emitted a *mrrf,* which meant, *We should be so lucky.*

I said, "Of course not. We need your help."

Sophie grinned. "You sure do." Then she looked

at Bub. "Tell her about opportunity. Then we better get out of here, right? We've got detecting to do!"

Bub nodded. "I'm on it. Opportunity is in the way of *when* you do the crime. In this case, who could've been out and about in the middle of the night without anybody knowing? Now, Al here's got a wife, so if he got up and left, she'd rat him out."

"You better believe it," Al said.

"But ol' bachelors like me, there's nobody paying attention to what we're up to. Come to that, I've got a truck out there. So as of this moment, I'd say I'm your most likely suspect."

Eve shook her head. "I don't think so, Bub. You don't have a motive."

Bub looked at me. "The new kid is catching on quick."

At the same time, Al stood up. "This has all been very educational. But I gotta be going. Usually I get some relaxation time after the holiday rush, but not this year. I don't mind telling you, Eve, I've been run ragged with deliveries out to RSF-Z for your dad. Not to mention I'm up till all hours filling out paperwork for the hazmat permits he needs."

"What's RSF-Z?" I said. "What's hazmat?"

"RSF-Z is the storage facility the college built for Eve's dad," Al said. "And *hazmat*'s short for 'hazardous materials." If you want to haul certain chemicals, you need a permit from the state."

Sophie's eyes widened. "You mean like *dynamite*?" Sophie has always liked loud noise and destruction.

Al shook his head. "For dynamite, you need an explosives permit, and those are almost impossible to get. Hazmat covers things that aren't so volatile—things like bleach, or chlorine for a swimming pool."

Volatile—there was that word. Where had I just heard it? And what did it mean, again?

Al was putting on his coat when there was a thump on the porch, and a second later the door opened—right into him.

It was Officer Krichels. "Oh, sorry! Didn't see ya there."

Al winced and rubbed his face. "No worries. My nose was crooked anyway."

In Bub's living room, Officer Krichels picked up Luau, dropped him on the floor, and sat his long, skinny body down. Luau swished his tail (*Oh, yeah?*), jumped to the back of the recliner, and lay down behind Officer Krichels's head. That way he could keep watching his cowboy movie while at the same time batting Officer Krichels in the face with his tail.

"Nice to see you all," Officer Krichels said,

wiping cat fur from his face. "You're the new girl, right? Eve? How are ya?"

Eve said fine, thank you. Then Officer Krichels said, "Where's Yasmeen?"

This *where's Yasmeen* business was getting old, but luckily Bub explained that she had to practice for choir. In the meantime, I asked Eve if she wanted more soup.

Eve looked down at her empty bowl. "Oh, wow. I ate all that, didn't I? I never liked vegetables before."

"That'll happen," Bub said, because he knows his soup is the best. He was about to say more when his phone rang. It's an old-fashioned black one, with a bell and everything, so when I say *rang* I mean *rang*, and Bub even had to get up out of his chair and walk across the room to answer it.

Eve stared, then whispered, "Is Bub Amish?"

Sophie and I cracked up, and Sophie shook her head. "He's just Bub," she said.

I ladled two more bowls of soup. When I brought them back, Bub was still on the phone but not talking, and I realized that after "Hello," he hadn't said a word. Every once in a while, he opened his mouth, but it was no good. Finally, he got exasperated. "Excuse me? Who is this? Do I know you?"

This made whoever was on the other end laugh so hard I heard it through the receiver.

"Ohhh, sorry," Bub said. "Yes, of course, I—"

Bub shut his mouth. The person on the other end was worse than Sophie! Finally, Bub interrupted again. "Excuse me? But I think I've got the gist, and at this rate they'll be late before they even know they're wanted downtown. Thanks for calling."

He hung up the receiver and shook his head.

"Don't tell me," said Officer Krichels. "Angie Price."

Bub pointed at Officer Krichels. "Bingo."

That explained everything. Ms. Price is a dispatcher for the police department, and she also handles the phones sometimes. Talking to her can be, uh...an experience.

"Your mom asked her to call." Bub was looking at me. "She wants to know if you kids can be at the station at ten-forty-five—that's fifteen minutes. You would've had half an hour if that woman hadn't kept me on the phone."

"I can take you if you don't mind the back of a police car," Officer Krichels said. Then—courtesy of another encounter with Luau's tail—he had a sneezing fit.

"Don't you want some soup, Fred?" Bub asked.

Shaking his head, Officer Krichels stood up, then answered between sneezes. "I don't know why, but my allergies seem to be acting up."

Luau hopped down onto the seat of the recliner, tail still swishing. *I know why.*

Sophie swept the bits and pieces of calculator onto an old magazine and set it in the middle of the table. "I'll see to this later, if that's okay, Bub."

"No rush," Bub said. "It's been broken since along about 1985."

Meanwhile, Eve slurped the last of her soup, popped up out of her chair, and grinned. "This is so *exciting*! So far, I love fighting crime!"

Sophie looked at me and rolled her eyes. "Rookie."

CHAPTER TWELVE

Officer Krichels dropped Eve, Sophie, and me off at the College Springs Police Department. In the lobby, we could see Ms. Price at her desk on the other side of a sliding window, like in a doctor's office. She was on the phone. Ms. Price is round and has frizzy blond hair that she tries to keep in place with a headband. She likes clothes in pale colors like blue and pink and yellow, so she looks like she's wearing pajamas even though she's not.

"College Springs Police Department. We spring into action for you. Thank you for holding. May I help you?" she said into the receiver. Then she caught sight of us, grinned, and mouthed, "I'll be right with you."

The volume on the phone must have been turned up loud, because we could hear the caller's voice without being able to understand the words. It was a man, and Ms. Price looked annoyed. I guess a lot of people who call the police department have bad attitudes.

Ms. Price listened for a few moments, frowning.

Then she did something surprising—looked up at us and winked. After that she repeated exactly the same words she had said before: "College Springs Police Department. We spring into action for you. Thank you for holding. May I help you?"

The caller went ballistic. Ms. Price interrupted him. "No, as a matter of fact, I *didn't* hear a word you said. You were on hold, which is why I thanked you for holding. Perhaps you're not familiar with the concept of *hold*? It means you're there and I'm not. I might be on break. I might be dead. Oh—there's my other line. So sorry. Please hold for the next available operator, who, come to think of it, will be me."

Ms. Price pressed a button, put the receiver down, rubbed her ear, and smiled at us. "Let 'em learn a little patience. How are you doing, Alex? Long time no see! Hello, Sophie. Where's Yasmeen?"

Oh, great.

This time it was Sophie who said: "Practicing for choir auditions."

"Seriously?" said Ms. Price. "Well, Yasmeen was never short of nerve, that's for sure. And you are?" She looked at Eve, and I introduced the two of them.

"Very nice to meet you," Ms. Price said. "Any friend of Alex's and all that. Detective Parakeet is in her office. Besides me, she's the only one here today, even though we've got crazy nutballs"—she looked at the phone—"calling us nonstop. Take this guy—he hasn't left us alone since before Christmas, claims there's poison bombs on the highway and we're not doing enough to—"

"Angie?" Mom appeared on the other side of the window behind Ms. Price's desk.

Ms. Price swiveled around. "Yes, Detective?"

"Could you buzz the kids in, please? Then set up that video call to Belleburg. Mr. Yoder is expecting it. Who"—she nodded at the blinking lights on the phone—"have you got on hold? We're still waiting for Mr. Glassie, right?"

"Mr. Glassie, the director of the Ice Carnival?" Ms. Price looked down at the phone on her desk and shrugged. "Could be he's on hold. I haven't had a chance to pick up all the lines. As for the one I did, I don't think it would be wise to name names in front of the children, Detective, do you?"

"You mean it's our tipster?" Mom asked.

Ms. Price nodded. "Right. It's that crazy Professor—Oh, shoot, oops!" She looked at us again.

Mom sighed. "He's not crazy. He's just afraid of losing his funding, like everyone else at the college. Try to be polite, okay? Then find out what's become of Mr. Glassie, and go ahead and set up the conference call."

"All that?" Ms. Price said.

"Yes, Angie. All that," Mom said.

Ms. Price sighed a long-suffering sigh, then buzzed us in. We followed Mom down the hall toward her office.

On the way, I thought about the tipster guy. He must be the same one Mom talked about two weeks ago, the day of the Jensens' party. But what was the rest of that stuff—poison bombs? And what did Mr. Glassie have to do with anything?

In Mom's office, I noticed she had a copy of the *Middle Daily Times* on her desk. On the front page was a big headline about something called fracking.

"Where's Yasmeen?" Mom asked.

This time Sophie and I said it together: "*Practicing for choir auditions.*"

Mom held up her hands. "Okay, okay. Just asking. I hope she makes it, then. Usually she loves—"

"Detecting," I said. "Yes, Mom. We know. Anyway, Eve is getting the hang of this really quickly."

"Excellent," Mom said, "because this is a remarkable crime, one that must have been executed with military precision. Still, we are lucky in one respect. There have to be plenty of people who know what happened. The thief only had a short window of opportunity to take all those statues, or he would have been spotted. Our extra Ice Carnival patrols were going through town every half hour. The thief must have had help, and lots of it."

Sophie, Eve, and I looked at each other. What was she talking about? *All* those statues?

Mom touched her hand to her cheek. "Oh my goodness," she said. "It's been such a crazy morning. I forgot I haven't even had a chance to tell you."

"Tell us what?" Sophie said it before I could.

"It's not just Ice Eve that's missing," Mom said. "It's all the Ice Carnival statues—eighteen of them."

CHAPTER THIRTEEN

We had a million questions. But Mom said there was no time. There were only five minutes till the video conference with Mr. Yoder.

"But who's Mr. Yoder?" I asked. "And why are we even here?"

Eve answered the first part. "Mr. Yoder's my uncle."

Mom nodded. "And you're here because you're investigating the disappearance of Ice Eve. There's got to be a connection between it and the thefts downtown. Since it's a couple of hours round-trip to Belleburg, we're saving time with this video conference thing."

"But what does my uncle know?" Eve asked. "You don't think he's a thief, do you?"

"No, not really," Mom said. "And if I knew what he knows, I wouldn't have to talk to him. Since all the sculptures came from his studio, it seems like a good place to start. And there's something else, too."

"What?" I asked.

"Izzy Glassie is threatening to shut down Ice Carnival if we don't get the sculptures back. Except for Mrs. Miggins, the downtown merchants are in an uproar, and that means the chief of police is, too."

Ms. Price shouted from the conference room. "I need some help in here!"

Mom said, "Oh, dear," and we all got up and went down the hall. Ms. Price doesn't have any more skill with electronics than she does with old-fashioned telephones, and when we got to the conference room the whole place seemed to be possessed by demons. The TV screen that drops down from the ceiling kept rising and falling, the laptop on the long table flashed blue-to-black-to-blue, and an ominous hum pulsed from the wall speakers.

Without a word, Sophie held out her hand to Ms. Price, who gave her the remote control. Sophie studied it for a second, then pressed some buttons. Right away the TV was still, the hum was gone, and the laptop displayed its usual icons.

Mom and I are used to this, but Eve said, "Wow."

Next Sophie sat down at the laptop and asked, "What's your uncle's name and screen ID?"

"James Yoder," Eve said, "but I don't know any-thing about an ID."

"I'll look it up." Sophie tapped some keys, and

a photo of a bearded man—Eve's uncle—filled the computer screen.

"How did you *do* that?" Eve asked.

Sophie started to explain, but I tugged both earlobes, so she stuck out her tongue instead. "*Fine.*" Then she pressed another button, and this time Eve's uncle, live and in person, appeared on the TV above us. He was blinking as if he wasn't sure how he'd gotten there himself.

"Hello?" Mr. Yoder said. "College Springs PD— are you there?"

"We are here!" Angie Price said. "Where are you?"

"Here," said Mr. Yoder.

Ms. Price looked around the room. "No, you're not."

"I mean I'm in my studio in Belleburg," Eve's uncle Jim said.

"Well, there's your problem," Ms. Price said. "Because Belleburg is actually *there.*"

Mom rolled her eyes. "Angie? We can take it from here. Nice to see you, Mr. Yoder. As you've heard, there's been some trouble. This is a case we need to solve quickly, and we hope you can help."

The view we had of Mr. Yoder's studio showed him next to a counter with a sink in it. Behind him was a window that looked out on a driveway and a water tank.

"I hope so, too," Mr. Yoder said. "Bad enough the weather's been so warm this year. Then to have the sculptures go missing...It boggles the mind! Who would want them?"

"That's just what the police want to know, Mr. Yoder," Mom said. "Can you think of any reason anybody might to do this?"

Mr. Yoder shrugged. "Because they're setting up a competing carnival somewhere? Because they flat out don't like ice carnivals? But who doesn't like ice?"

Eve whispered to me. "This case is easy! It must be that toy store lady!"

"Maybe," I said, but in reality I couldn't believe Mrs. Miggins would go to the trouble of stealing eighteen sculptures—nineteen, if you counted Ice Eve.

"Mr. Yoder, I have a question," Sophie said. "How much does each of the ice sculptures weigh?"

"Anywhere from two hundred to a thousand pounds," he answered. "For the big ones, you need a hoist to lift them. The smaller ones, you can get away with a strong back and a hand truck."

"But you'd need a truck to get very far with one," Mom said.

"Absolutely!" Mr. Yoder said. "And you can only put about four in a pickup at a time."

"So I'm just trying to picture how this operation

took place," Mom said thoughtfully. "Someone who either had several trucks or one heavy-duty truck and a trailer stole into town in the middle of the night and, very efficiently, carted off all the sculptures. There had to be a swarm of people involved."

Mr. Yoder was nodding. "Young people, most likely, people with strong backs."

"Uncle Jim, I have a question," Eve said. "Are ice sculptures worth a lot of money?"

"Depends on what you mean by—" Mr. Yoder began, but his voice was drowned out by a dog's long, low howl. *"Marvin!"* He turned his head. "Cut that out right now!" The howling stopped, and Mr. Yoder apologized. "I don't know what's with ol' Marvin lately. He usually isn't interested in the studio at all, but these last few days he's been dying to get in here. Maybe there's a dead possum in the ductwork? Now, where was I?"

"Prices," Mom said.

"Ah, yes. Small ones are around two hundred fifty dollars, and the big ones are up to a thousand dollars. But when it comes to the College Springs Carnival, those prices are more in the realm of theoretical."

Mom frowned. "What do you mean, Mr. Yoder?"

"Only that the Carnival hasn't paid me for this year's yet. Or last year's, either, come to think of it.

78

It's not unusual for a client to be behind, but it's becoming a problem. I hope they get their finances worked out soon. Artists have to eat, too."

"Interesting," Mom said.

While Mr. Yoder had been explaining, a tanker truck had pulled into the driveway behind him. The truck was red, with a picture of a black Halloween cat and the words FRAIDY BROTHERS FRACTURING—WE SCARE UP THE GAS.

Uncle Jim heard the truck, turned to look out the window, and called, "Rudy? Can you...?"

A voice from offscreen said, "I got it, boss."

Mr. Yoder turned back to face us. "If you don't mind, I've got some cleaning up to do around here."

Mom looked at Eve, Sophie, and me. "Anything else, kids?"

While I tried to think, Mr. Yoder turned on the tap in the sink beside him. The faucct was just visible at the right of the screen, and as I watched, something strange happened—but it was so quick I couldn't sort it out.

First Mr. Yoder looked surprised; then he said, "Dang it—uh-oh..." and the screen flashed white. After that there was a *poof,* the sound cut off, and the screen went black.

CHAPTER FOURTEEN

Sophie frantically tapped the keyboard, looked at the TV screen, and tapped some more.

Ms. Price, who had been annoyed ever since she gave up the remote, said, "Hmmph. So much for the girl wonder of electronics."

"It wasn't me!" Sophie insisted, and a new display appeared on the laptop—a bar graph with wavy lines. Sophie studied it for a second and announced, "The link is fine at this end. Something must've happened at Mr. Yoder's end."

"Is my uncle all right?" Eve looked worried.

"I don't know," said Mom. "Angie, get him on the landline. Please? I've got the number here."

There was an old-fashioned phone in the middle of the table. Ms. Price pulled it over and dialed. After a moment, she spoke into the receiver. "Mr. Yoder? Angie Price at College Springs PD, we spring into action for you, calling on behalf of Detective Parakeet." (Pause.) "Okay, I guess, except for that problem with my knee." (Pause.) "You didn't? Well, it started last week—I sit at a desk all day, you see, and—"

Mom slapped her forehead, leaned across the table, and took the receiver from Ms. Price. "Mr. Yoder, Noreen Parakeet. What happened? Are you all right?"

Mom listened, nodded, and finally made the thumbs-up sign. Eve breathed, and Sophie said, "Must not've been fatal."

After Mom said goodbye, she explained that something had knocked a plug out of Mr. Yoder's computer. "Nothing to worry about, he said. We were pretty much done with the interview anyway."

"But what was that *poof* sound?" Sophie asked. "And did anybody else see a bright light?"

"I thought I did," I said, "but it all happened so fast."

"Some problem with the camera, I guess." Mom stood up. "Let's go back to my office, kids. We've got a few things to work out before we get on with the investigation. Angie, can you check on Izzy Glassie? He's really awfully late."

As Sophie, Eve, and I went back to Mom's office, I was thinking a crazy thought. Maybe Izzy Glassie wasn't late. Maybe he had stolen the ice sculptures, and now he was making his getaway!

I hadn't worked out this whole idea yet. But with his job, Mr. Glassie did have the means to steal the sculptures—a truck, the equipment, people—

and he had the opportunity. Nobody would think a thing about seeing him downtown in the middle of the night when Ice Carnival was going on. They would think he was just making sure everything was okay.

The thing I didn't get was the motive. Why would he want to sabotage an event he was in charge of?

Maybe it had something to do with the money the Carnival owed to Mr. Yoder?

By now, we were back in Mom's office, and she was laying out her plan for more investigating.

"Someone must have heard something last night," she said. "Almost no one lives downtown, but what about someone on Chickadee Court?"

"Bub heard a 'vehicle,'" Sophie said. "But none of the rest of us heard anything."

"I guess he doesn't know what kind of vehicle?" Mom said. "And he didn't look out the window or notice the time?"

"I don't think so, Detective Parakeet," Eve said. "I guess he didn't realize he might be an important witness."

"What about Mr. Stone?" Mom asked. "I know he has trouble sleeping sometimes. Or the Blancos? That dog of theirs must've waked up. Could I deputize you kids to go door to door on Chickadee Court and see what you can find out?"

Sophie and Eve said sure and stood up to go.

Meanwhile, I'd been thinking about my idea—and the more I did, the more I thought Mr. Glassie was definitely our prime suspect. More important, if Mom was going to nab him, she needed to act fast. She should be calling the highway patrol! The FBI! If he'd gone north, he and the ice sculptures could be in Canada by now. Maybe she should call the Royal Canadian Mounted Police!

"Mom!" I was excited. "I think I might've figured something out."

Mom used to think of me as a little kid with little-kid ideas. She never took me seriously. But things have changed since I solved those other mysteries. She pays attention. Now she sat back in her chair and looked me in the eye. "Okay, sweetie," she said. "Shoot."

But I never had the chance. I was just about to name our prime suspect, the one hotfooting it for the international border, when Ms. Price did it for me: "Mr. Glassie here to see you, Detective!" she yelled from the reception desk. "Can I send him back?"

CHAPTER FIFTEEN

Mr. Glassie is small for a grown-up man. He has a pointy nose and wire glasses. Today he was wearing plaid pants, nice shoes with tassels on them, and a black down vest over a long-sleeved turquoise polo shirt. He came into Mom's office, said "Hi-hi-hi-hi" to everybody, sat down in a chair, and then bounced back up and paced.

I could see from Mom's expression she was going to say something sympathetic about the sculptures, but before she could, Sophie blurted: "So how come you haven't paid Eve's uncle Jim in two years? He's a starving artist, you know!"

Mom, Eve, and I all said: "*Sophie!*" at various volumes.

Sophie shrugged. "This is no time for chitchat."

Mr. Glassie sat down and stood up again. "It's no secret the Carnival's finances are a shambles. Without the support of all the downtown business owners and the city, it's very difficult for us to prosper. That woman—"

"He means Mrs. Miggins," Sophie put in.

"We got that, Soph," I said.

"—has done a lot of damage. We don't have the money to do anything new, so people lose interest, so we lose money, so people lose more interest. Almost more than we need the sculptures back, we need an idea to get people excited about Ice Carnival," he said, then added, "A cheap idea."

Eve looked up. "Where I used to live in California..." Then she looked down again and said, "Never mind."

"No, tell us," I said.

"But you're all sick of California," Eve said.

"You're right," Sophie said, "but this is an emergency."

"We had a costume parade," Eve said, "to celebrate the winter solstice. You know, December twenty-first? Only, it was for pets. Everybody gathered at this park downtown with their pets in wild getups—like Hawaiian leis, and hats, and bows, and sweaters...The littler pets rode in wagons. Birds and big lizards rode on people's shoulders. There was music and then we paraded to City Hall. It was about a mile. So you could maybe do something like that. It's cheap and everything."

When no one reacted for a few moments, Eve looked as if she wanted to sink through the floor. This is a feeling I know well.

But then Mom said, "People here are crazy about their pets."

And Mr. Glassie said, "We could charge an entry fee."

And Sophie said, "It's brilliant. And the best part is we can pull it together in an afternoon."

Everybody looked at Sophie. "We can?"

"Two words." Sophie nodded. "Social media."

"She has a point," Mr. Glassie said. "Besides, the main downtown streets are already closed, so traffic control is easy. If we start at the college gates, we can end over on the north side of campus by the stadium."

Mom looked at me. "Luau is going to love it!"

I looked at Mom as if she had just sprouted antlers. Luau was going to hate it! He's much too dignified for a pet parade.

"Marshmallow won first prize two years in a row in California," Eve said.

"Okay, that you can put a lid on," Sophie said.

"We need prizes, and refreshments, and judges," Mr. Glassie said. "And we need them by six o'clock. Looks like I know what I'll be doing this afternoon."

"Who says the parade is at six?" Mom asked.

"I do," said Mr. Glassie. "Executive decision."

"What about the ice sculptures?" Mom asked.

"That's crime, and crime is your department,

right?" He was moving around Mom's office like a whirlwind. "Anyway, they were insured."

Mom looked up. "Oh?"

Insurance is something I know about from other cases. It means you pay a little bit of money to a company, and then, if something bad happens, like your house burns down or your ice sculptures get stolen, the company pays you a lot more money, enough to fix it.

This might seem like a bad deal for the insurance company, but it isn't. Most of the time fires and robberies don't happen, and they get to keep the money.

Mr. Glassie dropped back into his chair. "Don't look at me that way," he said to Mom.

"Well, to be honest, insurance does give you a motive for taking the sculptures," Mom said. "They disappear, you get paid, the Carnival's financial problems are fixed."

Mr. Glassie raised himself to his full height and puffed out his chest. "I have put my *life* into the Carnival," he said, "and I would never do anything to harm it! Now, let that be my last word on the subject. If we're going to organize a pet parade by six o'clock, there's a lot to do. Can you kids help out?"

"No problem," Sophie said. "And while we're at it, we'll solve the mystery, too. It's only one o'clock."

Eve looked at me. "Is she being sarcastic?"

I shrugged. "I can never tell."

During the next few minutes, we worked out all the parade details. We would charge a ten-dollar entry fee per pet, and there would be ribbons for the winners.

"I'll put an entry form up on our website," Mr. Glassie said. "You"—he pointed at me—"go over to the *Middle Daily Times* and tell that reporter, Tim Roberts, what's going on. You two"—he pointed at Eve and Sophie—"make a page for the social media sites. Also, ask your own friends and neighbors to participate."

Mr. Glassie would not take no for an answer. And maybe Sophie was sarcastic, but she was also right. If her mom picked her and Eve up now, they could go home, get on the Web, and interview the neighbors—all in an afternoon's work.

Meanwhile, I was going to tell Tim Roberts about the parade, then walk around and look at the storefronts where the sculptures used to be. Maybe the thief had left a clue.

"Can you give me a ride home after that, Mom?"

Mom nodded. "I've got a 'tipster' to talk to and some paperwork to finish up. So the timing should work out about right."

"Meet at my house at fifteen hundred hours to

plan our next move," Sophie said to Eve and me. "Is that a deal?"

Eve looked confused. "Fifteen hundred hours? What's that?"

Sophie rolled her eyes. "Three o'clock, *duh*. I see we still have some work to do to catch you up."

We all walked out of my mom's office together. In the lobby, Mr. Glassie said, "Thanks for the idea, Eve. I'm feeling a lot better about the Carnival now. Oh, wait — Alex. Before you go, I have been wondering about one thing."

"Yeah?" I said.

"Where's Yasmeen?"

CHAPTER SIXTEEN

In College Springs, the newspaper office is on Main Street, next door to the police department. This is lucky if you happen to be one kid trying to do two things—organize a costume pet parade and figure out who stole nineteen ice sculptures—at the same time.

Tim Roberts's desk is on the second floor in a sea of other desks, most of them empty. There used to be lots of reporters at the *Middle Daily Times,* but the paper doesn't make that much money anymore because—my dad explained to me—most people get news from TV or the Web. So visiting Tim Roberts at his office is a little like visiting a ghost town.

"Don't tell me. You're here about the ice sculptures," Tim Roberts said when he saw me coming.

"Hi, Tim. Very nice to see you. What's going on?" I always try to be polite—even when other people aren't.

"Busy," Tim said. "I'm working on a twenty-part series on hydraulic fracturing, also known as fracking. Did you see my piece in the paper today?"

"My mom did." I remembered it on her desk.

"How'd she like it?" Tim asked.

I had no idea. I hadn't asked. "She loved it," I said.

"Good! I'm hoping it will win some big award and be my ticket out of here."

"So, have you found out anything about the sculptures?" I asked.

Tim Roberts shook his head. "I haven't even had time to look into it yet."

"There's something else, too," I said, and I explained about the costume pet parade. "Do you think you could put something up on the paper's website? Mr. Glassie would appreciate it."

Tim said, "Why not?" and swiveled around to face his computer monitor. While I gave him the details, he typed. Then he read what he'd written out loud so I could make sure he had the facts, punched his keyboard and announced: "There. It's live. I hope it generates some interest. I'll go down and take some pictures later when the parade entries are assembling. We could use the art"—Tim yawned, picked up his coffee mug, looked into it sadly, set it down again, then finished his sentence—"for tomorrow's paper."

I stood up to go. "Cool," I said. Then I noticed that the design on his mug was the same as on the truck that had pulled up behind Mr. Yoder's studio—a black cat with the words FRAIDY BROTHERS FRACTURING: WE SCARE UP THE GAS.

"Hey, where did you get that?" I asked.

To my surprise, Tim Roberts blushed. "You're right. I shouldn't've taken it."

"Huh? What do you mean?"

"In my defense, I had just dropped my old mug and broken it, so I really needed a new one," Tim said. "When these guys offered, I said sure—even though reporters aren't supposed to take gifts from the people they interview."

"Oh, wow—was that mug a bribe?" I asked.

"I hope not," Tim Roberts said. "The Fraidy Brothers seem like good guys."

"What do they do?" I asked.

Tim said he'd explain if I sat down a second. Since I was curious, I did.

Tim leaned back in his chair. "Okay, so underneath a lot of Pennsylvania and neighboring states is a kind of rock called shale that's porous. You know what that means?"

"Full of holes?" I said.

Tim nodded. "Tiny holes. But here's the thing about them. Trapped inside is gas, the kind that could be used for heat and electricity and other things. Now, up till recently, it was so hard to get the gas out of the holes, it wasn't worth it. But then engineers figured out a cheaper, simpler way to do it. They force water, sand, and chemicals into the rock to break it up—fracture it, in other words."

"So that's where the word *fracking* comes from?" I asked.

"Exactly," said Tim. "Once the rock is broken up, the gas can be piped to the surface and collected."

I remembered the tanker truck outside Mr. Yoder's studio. "So is it gas in the tanks on the Fraidy Brothers trucks?"

Tim shook his head. "In their trucks it's probably dirty water and chemicals, the liquid that's been used for fracking," he said. "The Fraidy Brothers and other companies suck that liquid up and take it away. Otherwise, it might pollute clean water underground. Here, I'll show you something funny."

Tim swiveled back to his computer, brought up a video clip, and pressed Play. The scene was a normal-looking woman in a normal-looking kitchen. She turned on the tap in her sink, and water came out. I looked at Tim like, *What's your point?*

But then something amazing happened. There was a *poof,* and all of a sudden the water stopped being water and turned into…a *flame?*

"Is that for real?" I said.

Tim Roberts nodded. "Sometimes gas or dirty water gets in a neighbor's well, so if there's a spark or something near the faucet"—he threw his hands in the air—*"kablooey!"* Then he laughed and shook his head. "It's funny every time."

"Flammable water." I shook my head. "I don't think I'd want to drink that."

"Yeah, kind of gives new meaning to the word *heartburn,* doesn't it?"

I got up to go. "Thanks for explaining. And thanks for your help with the parade, too."

"Don't mention it," said Tim. "Hey—I didn't even ask…"

Here it comes, I thought. *He's going to say: Where's Yasmeen?*

But he didn't. Instead, he asked if I was investigating the missing ice sculptures, too.

I wondered what he meant by *too,* but I didn't ask. I told him yeah, Sophie, Eve, and I were all helping out my mom.

He nodded. "Let me know what you find out." Then he peered into his mug again—still empty—and looked up. "Hey—I'll see you tonight before the parade. I bet Luau will look sweet when he's all dressed up in costume."

CHAPTER SEVENTEEN

Outside, I could see what Mr. Glassie meant about Ice Carnival not doing so well. There were a few people by the booths selling cider and pretzels. Otherwise, downtown College Springs was so quiet it was almost spooky.

I put my hands in my pocket, turned right, and headed down Main Street. Passing the entrance to Cloud Alley, I felt a chill as a gust of wind blew between the buildings. At the same time, I heard footsteps behind me and glanced back.

No one there.

But what was that purple shadow in the doorway of the apartment building?

Did it move? Or did I imagine it?

I turned my eyes ahead and kept going, walking a little faster. Was I being followed? How do you know if you're being followed?

Then I heard it again, definite footsteps. This time I didn't look back. Instead, I gave myself a pep talk: *Alex, you're being ridiculous. It's daylight and you're on the main street of your own town. Even if someone is behind you, it doesn't mean they're following you.*

The pep talk made me feel better, and that was when I realized part of the problem. I was all by myself, and I'm not used to it. Usually, Yasmeen is with me. What I really wanted to do was turn to somebody and talk about the case. So I did the next best thing. I talked to myself. I don't mean out loud (*duh!*) but in my head.

—*So, Alex, you want to know what's bugging me most about this case?*
—*Sure, Alex, what?*
—*It's motive, Alex. Why would anybody want ice sculptures?*
—*Maybe there's some other Ice Carnival somewhere, an Ice Carnival even more broke than ours, and the thief couldn't afford to buy sculptures so he stole some.*
—*You have a good idea there, Alex. But if there was another Ice Carnival, there would have to be publicity for it, and if there was publicity, we would've heard.*
—*Why, that's an excellent point, Alex.*
—*Thank you, Alex.*

One thing I noticed about talking to myself: There was a lot of encouragement and not much argument. In that sense, it definitely beat talking to Yasmeen.

By now I had arrived at the Knightly Bank, where a little printed sign, DOLLAR SIGN, marked the space where the sculpture used to be. I looked at the empty space, then looked up and out over the street.

—*So, Alex, if you were trying to steal a bunch of sculptures at once, how would you do it?*

—*Hmm, Alex. Let me try to think like a thief. I guess what I'd do is park one big truck in the middle of downtown, get a whole mess of people and a whole mess of dollies, and fan out.*

—*Yeah, Alex. Downtown isn't that big. If everybody moved fast, you could do it in a few minutes.*

—*How long did Mom say it was between cop patrols?*

—*Half an hour.*

—*But what if there was someone else downtown to see you? Someone besides the cops?*

—*Unlikely, Alex. It's the middle of the night in December. Besides, Bub always says when people act like they know what they're doing, they generally don't get questioned.*

— You know what, Alex? That makes me think whoever committed this crime was someone with a lot of confidence, a class president kind of person.

— Yeah, you could be right — a person like Yasmeen, in other words.

— Oh, come on, Alex. What would Yasmeen want with ice sculptures?

— I'm not saying she stole the ice sculptures! I'm just saying someone like her stole them. What did Mom say? "Military precision"? Who do we know with military experience?

— Good question, Alex. There's probably a lot of people, but the only ones I know are Bub and Sam Banner, my old baseball coach. I don't think either of them would want a bunch of ice sculptures, though.

Here is another thing I learned that day about talking to yourself, at least in public. It makes you look strange to the outside world. How I know is because right about then a voice behind me said, "Alex? Son, are you all right?"

I was so surprised I probably jumped a mile. Then I turned and saw that it was my other baseball coach, Coach Hathaway. He's kind of an old hippie, with long hair and a little gold earring, but he's a good coach and I really like him.

"Hey!" I grinned. "How ya doin'? Six weeks till pitchers and catchers."

Coach and I bumped fists, and he asked me what I was up to. I didn't tell him I was talking to myself. I just said I was downtown helping my mom with the case of the missing ice sculptures. Then I added, before he could ask, "Yasmeen is busy practicing for choir auditions."

"So I hear," Coach Hathaway said. "And I hear you have a new friend, too, Eve Henry. I'm interested in her dad's research into grassoline. Green technology—that's where it's at. In fact, our good friend Coach Banner might be investing big-time in Professor Henry's work—and PYB is getting involved, too."

PYB is Pennsylvania Youth Baseball, the league I play with.

"That's interesting," I said, even though it wasn't *that* interesting. All I really cared about just then was the case. And while Coach Hathaway had been talking, I had noticed a wad of gray something that looked a little like sawdust on the ground by the DOLLAR SIGN sign. Could it have been dropped by the thief?

I bent down for a closer look and found —
ewww — that whatever it was had been chewed up.

"What are you examining, Sherlock?" Coach
Hathaway asked.

"I'm not sure." I bent closer. "Oh! Sunflower
seeds. Do you know anyone who chews sunflower
seeds?"

Coach Hathaway laughed. "Me, for one. You
know that, Alex. We played ball all season together."

I stood up again. "You didn't happen to steal
Ice Santa and spit this here for me to find later, did
you?"

Coach Hathaway laughed. "If I had, would I
be reminding you about my sunflower seed habit?
More likely I'd be trying to stomp on the evidence."

CHAPTER EIGHTEEN

Coach Hathaway went with me to look at a few more empty spaces where ice sculptures used to be. There were no more spit-out sunflower husks, and no other clues. I didn't feel like I was being followed anymore, either. But maybe that was just because I had company.

As we were walking back toward the police station, Coach Hathaway stopped and pointed at a clean, shiny pickup truck parked on the street. "Here's my ride," he said. "Can I take you somewhere?"

I looked at the truck. "No way that's yours! It doesn't even sag!"

Coach Hathaway laughed. "But it's got my bumper stickers, right? I just had it overhauled is all—and washed it, too. Gotta get the road salt off in winter or it'll rust."

"Now you sound like Coach Banner," I said.

Coach Hathaway grinned. "Next I'll be cutting off my ponytail. Hop in if you want a ride."

I explained about my mom, and he said I could

use his phone, so I called her. As usual, she still had work to do.

"Coach Hathaway has seat belts in that thing, doesn't he?" she wanted to know.

I pantomimed putting on a seat belt, and Coach Hathaway nodded.

"Yeah, he does," I said.

"Thank him for me, then," Mom said.

"Wait, Mom—one more thing," I said. "You need the results of my investigation, don't you? I found a wad of sunflower crud—the husks? It was by Knightly Bank, where the dollar sign was."

"So we might be looking for someone who chews sunflower seeds," Mom said. "Okay, it's better than nothing. Sophie and Eve phoned in, too. The neighborhood kids put up those flyers for you, so who knows? Maybe someone will call. And the girls found a few neighbors at home to interview. Several people were awakened around three-thirty, but nobody saw anything." She sighed. "We may just have to wait till somebody talks and word gets back to us here at the PD. It's bound to happen."

On the way to my house, Coach Hathaway told me more about his interest in green technology. It turned out that when the Banner family sold their lawn care business last year, they made some money, and they were planning to invest it in grassoline.

"Lawn care…grassoline. It fits, right?" he said. "I don't have money like the Banners do, but as I said, PYB might also get involved. Your average baseball field produces a high volume of grass clippings a year, clippings that have the potential to be made into—"

"Grassoline?" I picked up my cue.

"Exactly," said Coach Hathaway. "So PYB and Professor Henry are talking about a partnership, provided his project extends through baseball season."

"Why wouldn't it?" I asked.

Coach Hathaway turned the truck onto Groundhog Boulevard and looked at me sideways. "There's a rival project at Professor Henry's old college. They're trying to do the same thing, so it's kind of a race. Whoever wins gets the prize, the right to make and sell grassoline. It should mean a lot of money to investors and the college that backs the project."

"A race—wow. That's pretty exciting for something scientific," I said. "But what happens to the loser?"

Coach Hathaway made the last turn, onto Chickadee Court. "I don't think anyone can say for sure. But if it goes the wrong way for the home team, I wouldn't count on your friend Eve being around till baseball season, either."

* * *

Inside, I ditched my boots but didn't bother to take my coat off. I only had a few minutes before I was supposed to meet the girls at Sophie's. I could hear Dad in the kitchen, so I went in and explained that Coach had brought me home because Mom was working late.

"On her day off, no less—what else is new?" Dad was sweeping. "Did you find anything out downtown?"

"Lots, but not much about who stole the ice sculptures." I explained as quickly as I could—including the part about the costume parade. "Anything new here?" I asked. "Like a piece of pie I could grab before I head out again?"

"There's a piece of peach you can have. The filling didn't gel. Oh, and Yasmeen stopped by. She needed Luau for something."

"What?" I asked.

Dad emptied the dustpan into the trash. "I didn't ask questions. They were only gone a few minutes."

Yasmeen had borrowed Luau? Why?

I skipped the peach pie and went to find Luau. He was draped across the back of the sofa in the den, looking out the window at the six geese a-laying. In Luau's opinion, there is always the chance one will get up and run for it. If it does, Luau will be ready.

"Where'd Yasmeen take you, anyway? Are you okay?" I scratched him behind the ears.

Luau squinched his eyes, then bumped his nose against my palm. *So many questions, so few kitty treats.*

"If I give you one, will you tell me where you were?"

Luau attempted to roll over so I could scratch his belly, but he miscalculated and rolled off the top of the sofa, and then…down, down, down, *bump*— onto the seat cushion. On the way he scrabbled for a foothold, which looked as if he was doing kitty bicycle exercises in the air.

Luau looked surprised when he landed—*whoa!* Then he did a quick face wash to recover his dignity. *I meant to do that.*

"Sure you did," I said, and went to get him a kitty treat.

When I got back, he was curled up on an orange-and-black afghan on the sofa.

"So, you've been hanging out with Yasmeen, huh?" I dangled the treat over his head.

Luau rolled over on his back. *She needed help, and you were downtown with your new best friend.*

I remembered what Mrs. Miggins had said— that Yasmeen was afraid she might be replaced. "Did Yasmeen say Eve's my new best friend?"

For a fat cat, Luau can be surprisingly quick.

Now he flipped over and swiped at the kitty treat, knocking it out of my hand. Then, before the treat knew what hit it, he pounced and soon was chewing contentedly. *Thanks, Alex. Yummy!*

"Oh, fine." Without another bribe, I'd never get more information out of him. And he so didn't need another bribe—not with that belly of his.

I went to get my coat. I'd be late to Sophie's, but I had to know. Why had Yasmeen borrowed my cat?

CHAPTER NINETEEN

Jeremiah was frowning when he opened the front door. This was not a surprise. But was I crazy? Or did he look even more sorrowful than usual?

"Hey, bud, how you doin'?" I said. "Is Yasmeen home?"

Jeremiah nodded. "It's bad."

"What's bad?"

"The la-la-la," he said. "Listen."

We were quiet for a second, and from somewhere at the back of the house I heard the sound of a piano, and with it a voice singing what was probably supposed to be scales but sounded more like off-key yodeling.

I winced. "That's how she practices?"

Jeremiah nodded. "For hours. I'm not sure I can stand it much longer." Then he brightened. "But she can't practice while she talks to you, right? So come on in. Stay awhile. I can make you a peanut butter sandwich with any kind of jelly or jam you want."

"I can't stay," I said, "but I do need to talk to her."

Jeremiah said, "Wait right here. I'll get her." Then he disappeared.

The Popps are neat and tidy people, but this time of year their front hall was cluttered like everybody else's—with coats, scarves hanging from hooks, gloves, and snow boots. I tried to stay on the mat by the door so I wouldn't track melted snow inside, but there were already puddles on the floor by Yasmeen's boots.

As an experienced detective, I knew those puddles meant she had been outside recently. Otherwise the water would have dried up in the warm house. Also, she must not have stayed on the sidewalk when she was outside. The sidewalk was mostly dry. At some point, she'd been walking in somebody's yard or another place where there was still some snow. But where had she gone? And had she taken Luau with her?

I took a quick look around to make sure no one was watching, then bent down to examine one of Yasmeen's boots. On the sole were a layer of melting ice, a few salt crystals, mud, blades of grass, and a tiny clump of something else, something gray-brown like sawdust...sunflower husks!

"Alex, what are you doing?" Yasmeen had come into the hall.

As I stood up, I felt myself blush. "Oh, hi. How's practicing coming?"

Yasmeen opened her mouth to answer, but at the same time her mom appeared in the hall behind her. "Alex, it's so nice to see you," she said. "Won't you come in for a minute? We have a guest who would like to meet you."

"Uh...okay," I said, thinking this was pretty weird. "But I have, uh...a meeting I have to go to. So I can only say hi." I slipped off my snow boots and left them by the door. Then I followed Yasmeen and Mrs. Popp.

The Popps' living room is all cream-colored—the walls, the sofa, and the carpet. Every time I go in there, I'm terrified I'll leave a smudge. Sitting on a cream-colored chair by the fireplace was the bearded man from the Jensens' disaster party. I remembered his name at the same time he stood and introduced himself: "Professor Enzo Olivo."

I said, "Very nice to meet you, Professor," and tried to think what I knew about him. He had had the fight with Professor Henry at the party, plus he was the petroleum guy quoted in Tim Roberts's story about grassoline—the guy who didn't believe grassoline would ever work.

"In fact, I believe we've met before," Professor

Olivo was saying. "But you were only a very small boy."

"We got to know Professor Olivo at church shortly after we moved here from Trinidad," Mrs. Popp said. "We've been friends all this time."

"It's nice to see you again," I said. "But...well, I have this meeting to go to now, and—"

"Actually, Alex," Professor Olivo said, "there was something in particular I wanted to say to you."

This was getting weird. What could Professor Olivo possibly have to say to *me*? "Uh..., okay. Go ahead."

"It's a bit awkward," said Professor Olivo. "The thing is, I was hoping you could ask your mother, Detective Parakeet, to meet with me."

At least it wasn't me he was interested in. "Sure," I said. "No problem. But you could ask her yourself. She works at the police department. The number is—"

"Two three five—nineteen fifty-two." Professor Olivo finished my sentence for me. "I know it very well, and in fact we have even had one meeting. But for some reason, she seems to be reluctant to meet again, and it is quite important."

I said, "Oh, okay. Then I'll deliver your message."

That's what I said, but at the same time, I knew if my mom didn't want to talk to someone, no message from me would change that. In fact, he must really have been bugging her. I mean, who knows the police department phone number by heart?

Only someone who calls it all the time, and...

Wait a minute.

For the next few seconds, I must've stood there frozen like an idiot. Because finally Mrs. Popp's voice interrupted my thoughts. "*Alex?* Professor Olivo said thank you."

Professor Olivo's face came back into focus. He looked puzzled.

"What?" I said. "Oh! I'm sorry. You're welcome. And now"—I looked over at Mrs. Popp—"I hope you don't mind, but like I said, I've got to get going."

Five seconds later I had said goodbye and was in the front hall stepping into my boots. Yasmeen was right behind me. "So, Alex, what was it you came over for?"

Since by then I was really late, there was no time for what Sophie would call chitchat. "Where did you take my cat?"

"Who says I took him anywhere?" she said.

"Uh...my *dad,*" I said.

Yasmeen backed down. "*Okaaay.* And how come you're in such a hurry?"

"I'm going over to Sophie's. We're detecting. You know, I think we're just about to crack the case."

III

This was a total exaggeration. But I was irritated.

"So I guess the new girl's detecting with you?" Yasmeen said.

"Yeah, she is, and she has a name, you know—Eve."

Yasmeen frowned. "So ask Luau, if you want to know where we went. Or don't you talk to your cat anymore?"

I finished Velcro-ing my boots and got to my feet. "He said to ask you."

Yasmeen rolled her eyes. "Oh, puh-leez, Alex. This talking to your cat thing was cute when you were little, but you're a big boy now. Isn't it time to grow up?"

CHAPTER TWENTY

That last comment, as my mom would say, was uncalled for, and I left the Popps' house without either getting an answer or saying goodbye to Yasmeen. All down the front walk I was thinking she would yell after me to apologize.

But she didn't.

There was one good thing. I hadn't had to explain why I was examining her snow boot. What were sunflower husks doing on the sole, anyway? I had seen that other sunflower crud downtown, but Yasmeen and Luau wouldn't have had time to go downtown.

At Sophie's house, her mom answered the door. Mrs. Sikora is tall and wears pink lipstick, sparkly rings on every finger, and pink nail polish. She's always going to either the spa or the salon. Like Sophie, she talks a lot. Also like Sophie, she's not as dumb as you first think she is. "Alex, sweetheart, nice to see you. Did you have a good holiday? I don't think I've seen you since the disaster party at the Jensens'."

"Hi, Mrs. Sikora. I did have a nice holiday, thank you. How was your holiday?"

Mrs. Sikora waved me inside and led me downstairs to the family room, all the time describing her Christmas, with emphasis on presents. It was like listening to one of those shopping shows you see while you're flipping channels.

"Mom!" Sofie was sitting on a plaid sofa with Eve. "You're talking his ear off!"

Mrs. Sikora has had plenty of practice ignoring her daughter. Now she winked at me and Eve before heading back upstairs. "Let me know if you need anything."

I was planning to tell Sophie she ought to be nicer to her mom—but first there was something else I wanted to say. See, for once I was kind of proud of myself. I had figured out who Mom and Ms. Price's persistent tipster was: Professor Olivo.

It had to be!

And that meant he was the one worried about poison bombs on the highway, not to mention his funding at the college. I didn't know what any of that meant, but I did remember that Ms. Price had slipped and said "Professor" when she was talking about whoever it was that was calling my mom. This town is full of professors. But professors who have the police department phone number memorized?

Eve and Sophie listened patiently while I explained. When I was done, Sophie said, "Very smart, Alex. And what does it have to do with the missing sculptures?"

"Uh...well, Professor Olivo doesn't like Professor Henry—and Eve is Professor Henry's daughter, and her birthday present was stolen. So that's kind of a connection, right?"

"*Okaaay*," Sophie said. "But even if a grown-up college professor would steal a kid's ice sculpture just to be mean—he wouldn't steal a whole bunch of other ice sculptures, would he?"

"Well," I said, "yeah. I'm not saying he's necessarily the thief."

"Good try, though, Alex," Sophie said. "But now we need to tell you what *we've* been doing all afternoon. We've been busy, haven't we, Eve?"

Eve nodded, but I noticed she looked a little traumatized. Hours alone with Sophie will do that to you.

Sophie started listing accomplishments. These included posting the particulars of the costume pet parade on the Web, then designing and sending e-mail invitations to everyone in their contact lists. Most kids RSVP'd right away.

That was the pet parade part of their assignment. As for detecting, I already knew from Mom that Sophie and Eve had interviewed the neighbors on Chickadee Court. Now Sophie filled in the details.

"The crime must have happened around three-thirty a.m.," she said. "Mrs. Snyder, Mr. Blanco, and Mrs. Swanson all heard someone driving on Chickadee Court at around the same time. Mr. Blanco figured it was the newspaper being delivered early. But then, when his dog kept barking, he went downstairs and saw somebody driving down Chickadee toward Groundhog Boulevard. There was no moon, but he thought it was a pickup truck, an old one with the round kind of bumpers. And he thought there was only the driver, no passengers.

"I asked him if there was something in the back—like a kid-sized ice statue of a girl—and he said he couldn't be sure but it was possible," Sophie concluded.

Now it was Eve's turn. She might be a little traumatized, but she definitely liked this detective thing. "The pickup truck didn't have any lights on!" she said. "Mr. Blanco thought that was strange, but he was half asleep so he didn't do anything about it, just went back to bed."

"Sounds like that must've been the thief, all right," I said. "It doesn't do us very much good, though. It's not like anyone got the license number."

"I guess not," Eve said.

She looked disappointed, so I quickly reassured her. "You did good! Better than me. I hardly found out anything—anything that has to do with Ice Eve, anyway." I thought of telling them what I'd learned about fracking from Tim Roberts, but it didn't seem relevant. I did mention I'd run into Coach Hathaway and he'd told me Coach Banner might be an investor in grassoline—and that grassoline might make a lot of money.

"Did you know that?" Sophie asked Eve.

Eve shrugged. "Dad doesn't talk that much about his work. I mean, I know the idea behind grassoline, but that's about all."

Then I said I'd seen some sunflower husks downtown and some more on the sole of Yasmeen's boot.

Sophie said, "Millions of people chew sunflower seeds, Alex."

"My dad used to chew sunflower seeds," Eve said. "But my mom thought it was gross with all the spitting, so he quit."

"Your dad could've left spit-out sunflower seeds in the neighborhood somewhere," I said. "But do you think he was downtown last night?"

Eve looked at me funny. "My dad worked at his lab all night. And he doesn't chew sunflower seeds anymore. And anyway, he can't be a suspect, can he? I mean, Ice Eve was a present to me from him and my mom."

She seemed upset, and I didn't want her to be. "No, no—no way. He's not a suspect. Because besides all that, he's your dad."

Eve bit her lip. "I should tell you something else then, in case it matters. We have an old pickup truck, the kind with round bumpers. Dad keeps it in the garage."

I shrugged. "Lots of people have old trucks."

"Still." Sophie tapped the side of her head. "We'll keep it in mind. Meanwhile, Alex, where did Yasmeen say she picked up the sunflower seeds on her boot?"

"She didn't say. We, uh...had a fight, sort of."

"Oh?" Sophie and Eve said at the same time.

"I don't want to talk about it."

After that, the girls started talking about the Chickadee Court neighborhood's entry in the pet parade. What were we going to wear? What were we going to do? How were we going to dress up our pets?

This was not a guy kind of conversation, and I was doing my best to stay out of it when I realized I hadn't even told Luau about the parade. I had been too distracted.

"What we need," Sophie said, "is a pet that can do tricks. But nobody has one of those."

"Yeah," Eve said. "Marshmallow's only trick is catching a Frisbee."

Sophie's eyes got big. "But that's perfect! We've all got light-up Frisbees, right? We can get the kids on Chickadee Court together and be a precision Frisbee team!"

Eve said she didn't have a light-up Frisbee.

Oh, shoot. Now what was I supposed to do? You're not allowed to tell about a birthday present in advance, are you?

But Eve looked sad, and it was kind of an emergency, so I told her what I'd gotten her from Mrs. Miggins's store...and she gave me a kiss on the cheek!

Oh. My. Gosh.

I don't even want to think about the color my face turned.

Sophie's expression said *Gross!* but she got over it fast and plain old rolled her eyes.

I was wondering if I was supposed to say something, like "Thank you," when luckily Eve's phone rang.

"'Unknown number,'" she read, and was about to hit Ignore when Sophie said: "*Answer it!* We put your phone number on the Ice Eve flyer, remember?"

"Oh, no—oh, right!" Eve fumbled for the ringing phone and almost dropped it, but finally recovered. "Hello?"

While Sophie and I watched, Eve's face turned from surprise to excitement to confusion and back again. Meanwhile, Sophie was going crazy. "What is it? Did somebody find her?"

Finally Eve took a breath, let it out, and said, "Okay, but I don't know where that—" She looked up at us, then frowned. "Hello? Hello?" She shook the phone, then looked at the screen again. "They hung up."

Sophie continued to go crazy. "Was it about the statue?"

Eve set her phone down, looked at me, then looked at Sophie, then grinned. "You guys," she said, "this is so exciting! I *love* detecting. Only, where's the house that's under construction on Groundhog Boulevard? Because whoever it was that just called says that's where we can find the missing lady!"

CHAPTER TWENTY-ONE

The three of us practically tripped over each other running up the stairs from the basement. At the same time, Eve was telling us about the phone call. The person had a breathy voice. Maybe whoever it was, was trying to disguise it?

"I don't know for sure if it was a man or a woman, or a little kid, even," Eve went on. "Where is this house?"

By then we were in the front hall, grabbing our coats and boots. "It's only around the corner." I stuffed my hands into my gloves. "But I better call my mom."

Eve shook her head. "That was the other thing the person said. No grown-ups."

"What?" It was my turn to shake my head. "I don't like that. It sounds weird."

"What—are you chicken?" Sophie asked.

Of course I'm chicken, I thought. *Aren't all sensible people chicken?* Then I thought of something else. "Wait a sec. They said 'missing lady'? Not 'ice sculpture' or anything like that?"

Eve thought for a second. "Hunh-unh," she said finally. "But what else could they be talking about?"

Sophie pushed the front door open. "Bye, Mom! We're going outside for a while. You're a grown-up, so don't try to follow us!"

"Take Byron with you!" Mrs. Sikora answered. And in the same instant Sophie's seven-year-old brother came flying down the stairs as if he'd been tossed.

"She's so not fair!" he whined. "All I asked was can I play underwater darts in the bathtub…Where are we going?"

None of us especially wanted Byron, but arguing would take too long. "Get your coat," Sophie said. "We'll explain on the way."

To get to the unfinished house, you cross Chickadee Court, walk to the Jensens', and turn right on Groundhog. The sidewalk in front had been shoveled, but the yard was only a dirt patch covered with sloppy ice and mud. Leading across it was a path of cruddy old plywood boards. We followed the path, slipping and sliding, to the front entrance, which was about four feet off the ground. There weren't any steps—there wasn't even any door—so we had to jump and climb up the bare wood to get inside. Byron was too short, so Eve and I knelt down, grabbed him under the arms, and lifted.

"Everybody good?" Sophie said when we were all inside. "All right then, troops, fan out! Eve—you take the kitchen and family room." She pointed randomly behind her. "Alex, you go upstairs." She pointed randomly up. "Byron"—she pointed randomly at Byron—"your job is to stay right here and watch in case any bad guys come."

"Bad guys?" Byron's voice squeaked.

I shook my head. "Sophie, what are you talking about? What bad guys? And what upstairs? Do you see any stairs?"

Sophie looked around. "Whoever heard of a house without stairs?"

Eve said, "A lot of houses in California—" then stopped when she realized that Sophie, Byron, and I were all looking at her. "Never mind."

The house had no roof, only blue plastic sheeting, which made it feel dark and haunted inside, not to mention that it was cold and damp. The whole effect was spooky, and I for one did not want to wander around in the shadows by myself. "Let's just stick together," I said. "We can cover everything in like five minutes."

"Maybe not even that," Eve said, "because look." She pointed. Through a doorway ahead of us, we could see a mess of dark spots on the bare wood floor. Footprints? We went to investigate, and

Sophie used the flashlight on her phone to get a better look.

"They look like kid footprints to me," she said. "Byron, put your foot down next to that spot."

Byron squealed. "I didn't steal any ice lady!"

Eve reassured him. "We know you didn't, bud. You were home with us all afternoon. But we're curious if maybe the prints might belong to a kid—or kids."

Byron placed his foot, and sure enough, the prints were about the same size.

"If it's someone in the neighborhood, that makes it probably either Jeremiah, Billy Jensen, or Russell's little brother, Graham," I said, and then I thought of something. "Eve, did the person on the phone use the word *grown-ups*? Not *adults*? Not *parents*?"

Eve thought a second. "Definitely *grown-ups*."

"That's a kid kind of a word," I said, "so what I'm thinking now is this whole thing is a kid operation."

"Do kids in Pennsylvania drive trucks in the middle of the night?" Eve asked.

"Ha!" Sophie said. "She's got you there, bud. Now, does anybody else want to actually *find* Ice Eve? Or are we just going to stand here and chit-chat all day?"

You'd think it would be easy to follow footprints through an unfinished house, but I'm here to tell you that it's not. Pretty soon they started over-lapping themselves, and after that I'm afraid we might've started following our own prints in circles.

"Wait a sec," said Eve. "Isn't this is the laundry room? We've been here already."

"It's not the laundry room, it's part of the kitchen," said Sophie.

Eve pointed. "I think that's where the dryer goes."

Sophie shook her head. "Dishwasher."

Byron piped up. "Do I hear *toilet*?"

By then, we were all getting grumpy. It was cold and dark. The parade was supposed to start at six. What were we doing here at all?

"Look, can we all agree we're going in circles?" Eve asked. "I'm not even sure there is a missing lady—let alone Ice Eve."

Sophie put her hands on her hips. "Are you whining?"

Eve opened her mouth, but I spoke first. "Expressing your opinion is not whining."

Sophie started to say something, but from behind us came a sound like wood slapping wood, *crack*. Was it somebody climbing into the house the same way we had?

Who?

And after that there were three more sounds, all of them louder than the first—*crack, crack, crack!*—

that startled us all so much we did the dumbest possible thing—we scattered! And now, guess what, each of us was alone in the shadows in a spooky, dark unfinished house. My first thought was to yell, but I didn't want whoever had just joined us to know where I was and come after me. Then, out of the corner of my eye, I saw a purple shadow moving through what might be the living room.

Very slowly, I turned toward it, hoping to see better without attracting attention—but I couldn't. Should I follow it, or run away?

In the end, I didn't have to decide because someone screamed—Sophie!

Sophie is the bravest person I have ever met. So if something was scary enough to make her scream…the smart move would be to run fast in the opposite direction!

But what kind of friend does that?

"I'm coming, Sophie!" I hurried blindly toward her voice, bouncing like a billiard ball off half-built walls, and finally tripping over Byron, who was coming from the opposite direction.

Clatter, thud, grunt—ouch! Now the two of us spun around and kept going. Two steps later, we hit something hard—which promptly fell to the floor—*bang!*—and after that there was no sound but thumping hearts and panting.

"Wh-wh-what happened?" Byron squeaked. "Did we find Ice Eve?"

The answer came in a beam of light from Sophie's phone flashlight. Aimed at the floor, it shone first on a pair of painted pink lips, painted blue eyes, and finally a whole bunch of painted blond curls.

I not only recognized that face, I knew where I could find ten more exactly like it.

"She's a 'leven lady dancing!" Byron cried.

"And she scared the be-whatzit out of me when I ran into her, too," said Sophie.

Like the other human Twelve Days decorations— drummers drumming, pipers piping, lords a-leaping, maids a-milking—the ladies dancing are sort of like giant paper dolls, except they're made out of heavy, thick plywood. That's why, when Byron and I slammed into this lady in the dark, she made so much noise hitting the floor.

"So she's the missing lady?" Eve had come up behind me. "It was never Ice Eve at all?"

"I guess," I said.

Eve said what we were all thinking. "Why would anyone move her out of the Blancos' front yard?"

"I have no idea," I said.

"We'd better get her home and get to the parade," Sophie said. "Looks like somebody's played a joke on us."

The fastest way to the Blancos' was to cut through the Jensens' yard. Byron went ahead to make sure the way was clear. Eve took one dancing foot and Sophie the other. I took the smiling head. She wasn't that heavy, but the way the plywood was curved, it was impossible to get a good grip with our winter gloves on. After about two steps, we stopped to set her down, take our gloves off, and start over.

"Somebody else was back here, and it wasn't that long ago," Byron reported as he picked his way carefully through the mud and slush. "I keep stepping in footprints."

"Must've been whoever stole her in the first place," Sophie said.

"*Ouch*," I complained. "Is anybody else getting splinters?"

"Me," said Sophie.

"Me too," said Eve.

Mr. Blanco was standing in his front yard when we got there, facing toward the other ten ladies and away from us. He was nodding at each lady in turn, and after a second I realized what he was doing—counting. I couldn't help smiling. How many times had he gotten up to ten, thought he must've miscounted, and started over?

"Missing something?" Sophie called.

Mr. Blanco spun around, and at the same

moment the lights came on and the music started. *"On the first day of Christmas..."*

"We don't know, so don't even ask us." Sophie handed her corner to Mr. Blanco. "She was in the unfinished house around the corner, and here she is. Do you mind setting her up again? We're exhausted."

Mr. Blanco said, "What was she doing in the vacant house? Who took her there? How did you guys know—"

Sophie looked at me. "Was he not listening, or what?"

There was a lot to tell, so I talked fast about the flyer and the phone call and the kid-sized footprints in the unfinished house. Then I added, "But that's all we know. Do you need help setting her back up?"

"I can do it." Mr. Blanco took the lady dancing from me and Eve, then balanced her on an edge on the ground. "I'm just glad she's back. Thanks."

"You're welcome," I said.

Sophie tugged my arm. "Come on! We can't exactly be late to our own parade!"

"Oh, and Alex?" Eve reminded us as we took off for our houses. "Don't forget to bring my birthday present, too—you know, my new Frisbee?"

CHAPTER TWENTY-TWO

Eve's Frisbee, Eve's Frisbee, Eve's Frisbee—I repeated it every time my boots hit the ground on the jog home.

Through the front door, off with the boots, hi to Dad and grab the Frisbee...but first, since the parade was a costume pet parade, I needed a costume for my pet. And when I looked at the clock in our front hall, I realized I had approximately forty-five seconds to find one, then another forty-five to attach it.

I took the stairs two at once, wishing for the first time in my life that more girls lived in my house. Girls often own dolls, and doll clothes kind of fit if you put them on a cat.

Since the closest thing I have to sisters is Mom, I passed my bedroom door and kept going till I got to my parents'. Then, thinking silent apologies to Mom, I opened a couple of her dresser drawers, hoping for inspiration.

Aha!

Five seconds later, I was running back down the

stairs thinking that maybe, instead of growing up to be a firefighter or a comedy writer, I would grow up to be a costume designer for animals that star in commercials. That's gotta pay well, right? I mean, I think I just might have a knack for this.

In the den, I found that Luau hadn't moved from his spot on the afghan on the sofa.

"...*five go-old RINGS!*" the Christmas carol sang. "*Fo-ur calling birds, three...*" The sofa is by the window, so you can hear the song from there. During the holidays, it's the official sound track of life on Chickadee Court.

When I came into the den, Luau opened his eyes, stretched his paws, and looked up. In my hand was a silk scarf with pictures of lions on it. Luau yawned and probably would have made some kind of snarky comment, but I didn't give him time.

"Hold still, and don't ask questions," I said.

Luau blinked a slow blink. *Don't catnap victims get a last request?* Then he hiccupped, which was kind of strange, and squinted, which meant, *Excuse me.*

"It's only temporary," I said. "I should've told you sooner, but it's been a crazy day." Fiddling with the scarf and a big pin made of red fake jewels, I explained about the parade. "You're going as king of the jungle. Maybe you'll win a prize. You'd like that, right?"

Luau didn't answer, just hiccupped again. Meanwhile, I kept trying to adjust the pin until—"Ow!"—I pinned myself. Luau didn't say anything to that, either. *He must really be annoyed,* I thought.

"Okay, sorry, but you gotta stand up or I can't get this straight. I should be able to make a crown out of something, right? But for now, see, this is your cape." I grasped Luau under his front legs and tried to pull him up, but he wouldn't pull.

That's when I looked into his face. His eyes were open, but they looked weird, as if they weren't aimed right. There were dribbles of cat spit on his chin. And his nose, which is usually pink, looked more like gray.

"Luau? Buddy? Are you okay?"

Luau looked up at me and focused briefly. *Not feeling so...* he started to say, and then he went limp.

"Dad!"

All kinds of horrible things went through my head while Dad was examining Luau. The main one was that I couldn't imagine life without my cat. We've always been together. We understand each other.

But then Dad stood up and said, "I don't know what's going on with him, but he's awake now, and his breathing is okay. Probably a virus or something. To be safe, I think I'll run him to the vet. Do you want to come?"

I nodded. "I'll call over to Eve's and tell her I can't go to the parade."

"Oh, hey, wait—I forgot the parade," Dad said. "Look, you don't have to come to the vet. Luau's ordinarily a very healthy cat, so whatever this is, he'll fight it off. Mom's gonna try to make the parade, so I can call and tell her to tell you what the vet says. If she doesn't get there, I'll call Sophie."

"Really?" I felt bad about abandoning Luau when he was sick. But wouldn't I be abandoning Eve and Sophie if I skipped on the parade? And it wasn't an emergency with Luau, right? "Okay, you promise to call?" I stroked Luau's back and told him to get better. His answer was a weak-sounding *mrrff* that for once I couldn't translate.

CHAPTER TWENTY-THREE

Out the door I ran, past our swans and the Lees' geese, boots pounding the pavement. In the Henrys' driveway, their SUV was waiting with the motor running. I saw it…and at the same time remembered Eve's Frisbee.

Oh, cripes, they were going to kill me, but it would be worse if I didn't bring the Frisbee.

Without breaking stride, I made a U-turn. Two minutes later, I was heading back toward the Henrys' with Eve's birthday present under my arm.

What a day! I had been late to every single thing so far—and now I was late again.

Eve, Sophie, and Eve's mom were in the car waiting. Marshmallow was barking in a pet carrier in the back. *Let me out of here!*

"Where's Luau?" Eve asked as I climbed into the backseat next to Sophie.

"And why do you keep being late?" Sophie wanted to know. "I had about a half a zillion things to do when I got home, and I got here on time, and now you didn't even remember your very own cat, and I really think you—"

I tugged my earlobes, but Sophie kept right on talking. Finally, she had to breathe, and I apologized and explained about Luau. I admit I made him sound a little more deathly sick than he actually was so Sophie would shut up about me being late.

It worked, too, because then everybody got all worried and made a bunch of poor-kitty comments, and I had to reassure them. "He'll be okay."

Then I changed the subject by handing Eve's birthday present to her up in the front passenger seat.

When she took it, she acted kind of girly. "*For me?* Oh, that's so sweet, Alex. You shouldn't have."

Next to me, Sophie pretended to stick her finger down her throat.

Meanwhile, Eve unwrapped her gift and squealed. "Oh, Alex! I just totally love it!"

"Uh...you knew what it was already," I said.

"Ye-e-es," she said, "but it's still special."

Mrs. Henry made the right turn from Chickadee onto Groundhog. "A Frisbee like that is a great gift, Alex," she said. "The girls told me about your plan for a parade entry. I'm sure it'll look terrific."

"Do you think anybody else is even going to show up?" Sophie asked. "It's going to be kind of depressing if it's just the three of us playing Frisbee toss with Marshmallow."

"On the plus side," I said, "we'll win all the ribbons!"

"Hey—you're right," said Sophie. "This is a win-win situation! What's Marshmallow's costume, anyway, Eve?"

"He's going as a little white dog with a sparkly red bandanna," Eve said. "It was the best I could do on short notice."

"It's brilliant," said Sophie.

"Sophie, could you be done with the sarcasm?" I said.

"What sarcasm?" Sophie said.

"And anyway, the bandanna has sparkles," Eve pointed out.

"Is there an update on the case, guys?" Mrs. Henry asked. "You've been so busy all day, Eve said you'd tell me in the car."

On our way down Groundhog, we told about the video conference with her brother, Mr. Yoder, and about the sunflower seed crud. Then I said we'd figured out that whoever stole the ice sculptures downtown must have been super-efficient and well organized because he or she didn't have very long between police patrols to pick up the sculptures and haul them away.

And the girls explained what the Chickadee Court neighbors had seen and heard.

When Sophie mentioned the part about the Blancos' dog barking, Mrs. Henry laughed. "Marshmallow must've been asleep on the job."

Eve looked over her shoulder at Sophie and me. She was frowning. "Yeah, that's strange," she said. "Marshmallow usually always—"

But what Marshmallow usually always does, we'll never know, because Mrs. Henry said, "Hold on!" and braked suddenly, causing us all to lurch forward against our seat belts, and Marshmallow to yip furiously from his crate. "Sorry," said Mrs. Henry. "What's with all this traffic, anyway?"

Sophie waved her arms as if she could clear a path. "We are in a hurry! *Move, people!*"

"They can't hear you, Sophie," I pointed out. "Only *we* can hear you."

Mrs. Henry said, "Maybe there was an accident. Did you find out anything else?"

"Not really," I said. "I mean, we went over to the unfinished house and rescued a lady dancing, but I don't think she had anything to do with Ice Eve. I think somebody was just messing with us."

Mrs. Henry nodded. "I see." And from the way she said it, you could tell her point was really: *You kids have had a whole day to work on this, and you haven't made much progress, have you?*

CHAPTER TWENTY-FOUR

I have been a kid for more than eleven years, and one thing I've learned is it's mostly a waste of time to argue with grown-ups. Now, though, I had no choice. I had the most detecting experience of anybody in the car. I needed Sophie's and Eve's help to solve the case. And I didn't want the two of them to get discouraged.

"Well, actually, Mrs. Henry," I said politely, "when you're working on a case, there is always a moment like this, a moment when nothing adds up, and it seems hopeless, and you want to quit. But then you do a little more work, and all of a sudden—when you least expect it—things start to make sense."

Inching the car forward, Mrs. Henry glanced at me in the rearview mirror and flashed a smile. "So if you weren't going to the parade," she said, "what would you be doing next to solve the mystery?"

I thought about that. "Probably writing out a list of suspects."

The car came to a complete stop again. Sophie

slumped back and frowned. Eve said, "So let's talk about suspects."

"Do you have suspects?" Mrs. Henry asked.

"There're *always* suspects," Sophie said, cheering up a little. "I think Mrs. Miggins did it."

"Sophie, you know that's not how it works," I said. "You don't just pick somebody you don't like and announce that's who did it. You have to be objective and use reason!"

"And you have to think about means, motive, and opportunity," Eve said.

"Oh, hogwash," Sophie said. "Sometimes you just make a good guess."

"Okay, fine, Sophie," I said. "Why Mrs. Miggins?"

"Motive: She doesn't like Ice Carnival," Sophie said. "Means: She has a truck—she needs one for her store. Opportunity: She lives by herself except for Leo G. So for all anybody knows, she was running around all over town last night, stealing ice sculptures."

"But why did she steal Ice Eve?" I asked.

Sophie shrugged. "Because she wanted the complete set?"

Eve and Mrs. Henry laughed.

Sophie frowned. "I wasn't trying to be funny."

Mrs. Henry made the right onto Main Street—but the traffic didn't let up.

Eve said, "Do I get to pick now? Because I say Mr. Glassie. His motive is to get the insurance money for the Ice Carnival. His means is the trucks they used to haul the sculptures in the first place. And opportunity? Well, nobody would think a thing about him being downtown during the night. Even if he got caught, he could just tell people he was moving the ice sculptures around."

Sophie nodded. "Pretty good for a rookie. Plus I don't like those little glasses of his or the way he bounces around all the time. Case closed. He did it. Except—well, I do have another suspect: Coach Banner!"

"*What?*" I said.

"*Who?*" Eve said.

"Would that be Sam Banner?" Mrs. Henry asked. "Tom and I met him and his wife at an event a few weeks ago when we came out to visit. They were planning to invest in Tom's technology—in grassoline."

"And did they?" Sophie asked. "Invest, I mean?"

Mrs. Henry winked at us in the rearview mirror, which seemed to mean yes. But then she said, "I'm not supposed to talk about it."

Sophie was nodding. "*Oh,* yeah. Sam Banner used to be in the army, so he's good at organizing junk. He used to own a lawn care company, so I bet he's probably still got trucks and equipment—"

"But what about motive?" I asked.

"Money," said Sophie simply.

"What money?" I asked.

"I'm still working on that part," Sophie said. "But which sculpture disappeared first? Ice Eve! And Ice Eve's dad is the inventor of grassoline. And grassoline is going to make money—"

"We hope!" Mrs. Henry interrupted.

Sophie nodded. "Exactly. So there you have it— all neatly tied up and connected, uh...somehow."

"But don't you have it backward?" I asked. "Sam Banner wants grassoline to succeed. That makes him in favor of Professor Henry."

"More likely," Eve said, "somebody who *didn't* like my dad or my family would steal Ice Eve. Like Yasmeen's family. Hey—and besides that, they're friends with that crazy Professor Olivo guy. And we know he doesn't like my dad or his research."

"Yasmeen and her family would never steal anything," I said.

"What happened to being objective?" Sophie asked.

"Give me a break, Sophie," I said. "You've known Yasmeen almost as long as I have. Anyway, this whole thing can't be about Eve's family. Because that wouldn't explain the ice sculptures downtown."

Sophie closed her eyes. "This must be the part where I always get a headache."

"Hey, you guys—what about this?" Eve asked. "Maybe we've been looking at the whole thing the wrong way. Maybe instead of trying to figure out who took the ice sculptures, we should be trying to *find* the ice sculptures. Whoever took the sculptures had to put them someplace, right? Someplace big if they're all together, and someplace inside to hide them."

Sophie sat up as if now she was paying attention. "Also, wouldn't it have to be someplace cold? Otherwise, the sculptures would get all melty."

"I know a place like that," Mrs. Henry said. "And I know something else, too. It'll be faster for all of us to walk to the college gates from here. So I'm gonna make a right turn and park in the lot. Okay?"

We all agreed. It was only a few blocks to the college gates, and we didn't have anything much to carry.

"What place do you know that's like that, Mom?" Eve asked as the SUV came to a stop.

"RSF-Z." Mrs. Henry pulled the key out of the ignition. "You know—your dad's storage facility out beyond the stadium. The *R* stands for *refrigerated*.

The college built it for him because some of the chemicals he uses to make grassoline are volatile at warm temperatures."

Volatile. There was that word again. I couldn't remember exactly what it meant. But Sophie's uncle Al had said something about delivering hazmats—hazardous materials—out to Professor Henry's facility, too. Were those the same chemicals Mrs. Henry was talking about?

CHAPTER TWENTY-FIVE

You know the rare College Springs traffic jam that forced us to park five blocks from the start of the parade?

It wasn't caused by an accident at all.

It was caused by the crowds of people coming to the first annual Ice Carnival Costume Pet Parade!

We figured it out when we finally got to the college gates and saw how many people were already there. Sophie high-fived Eve. "We must've done really great on the publicity!"

Besides a ton of parents and kids and pets wearing crowns and coats and sweaters and cowboy hats, we saw Tim Roberts taking pictures, and Mr. Glassie, who gave us a thumbs-up. We also ran into Mrs. Miggins and Leo G., who was wearing a black bow tie around his neck.

Amazingly, Mrs. Miggins was smiling. "In one afternoon, my store sold out of doll clothes and kid costumes, too," she told us. "It was almost as good as Christmas. If the parade becomes an annual event,

I'm going to have to rethink my feelings about Ice Carnival."

The college gates are two stone pillars connected by a black iron arch. Under the arch the Ice Carnival people had set up a folding table, where volunteers were taking entry forms and money. Mrs. Henry turned to Eve, Sophie, and me. "You guys go ahead now and find the other kids you're marching with. I'll fill out your entry form and turn it in."

"Thanks, Mom!" Eve said.

We turned to go, but Mrs. Henry called us back. "Wait—what's your Frisbee team called?" she wanted to know.

This was a moment when I really missed Yasmeen. She would have had a name on the tip of her tongue. But Eve, Sophie, and I looked at each other like—*Yikes, I have no idea.*

It was Sophie who stepped up. "The Chickadee Court Precision Light-Up Frisbee Team. Okay?"

Eve and I looked at each other. "Okay."

Then, with Marshmallow following on his leash, we set out to find the neighbors. The first one we came to was Jeremiah, who told us Yasmeen couldn't come.

This was not a surprise, but I still felt disappointed. Usually, Yasmeen would have loved an event like this, one that offered so many opportunities for her to boss people around.

How long was she going to be mad at me, anyway?

After Jeremiah, we found Billy and Michael Jensen, Toby Lee, Ari, Russell and Graham, Kyle Richmond, and Byron. The Jensens had brought a couple of their friends, and Ari had, too, so altogether there were a lot of kids on our team, plus one grown-up, Marjie Lee. She had to be there to watch her son Toby because he's just little. Also, he's what my mom calls a holy terror.

"Okay, people, listen up!" Sophie shouted. "Who besides Eve brought a pet?"

Kyle raised his hand. He had brought his black cat, Halloween, in a wagon. There was an orange bow tied to Halloween's tail, but the way he was wiggling, you could see that the bow wouldn't be there long.

"Nobody else?" Sophie yelled.

Ari said, "It's too cold for my iguana," and Graham said, "I've only got a goldfish," and Russell said he'd left his dog, Myrtle, home because she's got arthritis and can't chase a Frisbee.

"Okay, people, fine," said Sophie. "So we're gonna focus on the Frisbees. Now, here's what we're going to do. I want you to line up in three rows of four—"

Jeremiah frowned, tugged Sophie's sleeve, and said, "We can't."

Sophie looked down at him. "Why not?"

"Because there's fourteen of us, and three lines of four equals twelve."

Sophie shook her head. "Seriously? Arithmetic at a time like this?" But she turned back to the rest of us kids and said, "So line up any way you want. Then what we do is toss the Frisbees. Who's got one?" About half the hands went up. "Okay—great. That's enough. And Marshmallow here—where's Marshmallow?"

Eve held Marshmallow up high so everyone could see. Marshmallow yipped: *Yikes—put me down!*

"Marshmallow's our Frisbee dog," Sophie explained. "You can tell by the bandanna, even though he's puny. So what we're gonna do is toss the Frisbees to each other, and when we miss, he'll get on out there and retrieve. Everybody got that?"

Everybody did.

"So now we should practice, right?" Eve said.

Sophie shook her head. "What are we—*wimps*? We're just gonna do what comes naturally and blow the pants off all these other entries. I mean, who's got light-up Frisbees? Us...or them?"

CHAPTER TWENTY-SIX

I don't know if you've ever been part of a precision light-up Frisbee team marching in a costume pet parade in Pennsylvania in late December.

But in case you haven't, I'll tell you what it's like.

First, it's cold, so you have to get over that. Then, till your teammates get their rhythm going, you're afraid you're going to get decapitated by one of the zillion Frisbees flying at your head. Finally, if the Frisbee dog marching with you is little, you have to watch your step because otherwise you'll either trip or squish him.

Besides all that, though, what it's like is super-fun!

Mr. Glassie had recruited the College Springs Community Band to lead the parade. The song they played is called "Baby Elephant Walk." Later I found out that was because it was the only song they knew with an animal in the title.

Meanwhile, I was just grateful they didn't play "The Twelve Days of Christmas."

The Chickadee Court Precision Light-Up Frisbee Team had been assigned to march right behind the band. I would be in line with Marjie Lee and Toby on one side and Ari on the other. But we'd all be pretty far apart, so that when we tossed our Frisbees they'd have a chance to get airborne.

Since the traffic jam had delayed everyone, there was a lot of standing around before the parade started. Sophie and I were hanging together. Eve was sitting on the curb with Marshmallow in her lap. She was worried about something—I could tell from how her face was scrunched up.

Come to think of it, Eve hadn't said a word since she asked her mom about the storage facility—RSF-Z. I was wondering what was up with that when something Billy Jensen said got my attention. He was a few feet to my left with Jeremiah, and he was complaining about how his splinters hurt.

Splinters?

The second Billy said it, Jeremiah looked up, saw me, and tried to shush him.

Sophie had heard the two of them, too, and she pounced. "You mean splinters like the ones I've got—*and* Eve and Alex've got, too?" she asked.

"Nope," said Jeremiah. "Billy and I's splinters are totally different."

"Oh—so it's you *and* Billy," I said. "And where did you get them?"

Billy and Jeremiah looked at each other. Then Jeremiah answered very carefully. "We were doing a favor for, uh…somebody."

"Who?" Sophie asked.

This time Billy answered. "Uh…for somebody who asked us to do a favor for her. A certain person."

"A girl person, I guess." Sophie looked at me. "And did she have a name?"

"That's a silly question," Jeremiah said. "Almost everybody has a name."

I was getting exasperated, but—lucky for Jeremiah and Billy—that was when the leader of the Community Band blew his whistle.

At last! The parade was going to start!

Eve jumped off the curb and let Marshmallow off his leash. Sophie hurried position herself where all of us could see her. Then, after a drumroll from the band, the first notes of "Baby Elephant Walk" sounded. Sophie stepped left, stepped right—marching to the beat—and as she did she raised her fist and counted: "One-two-THREE-four-FIVE-six-seven-*TOSS!* One-two-THREE-four-FIVE-six-seven-*TOSS!*"

And just like that, we were a precision light-up Frisbee team for real.

Light-up Frisbees light up only when they're spinning and go dark when they stop. For us, this meant that every eight steps, flying streaks of light whizzed among us, then it got dark, then it lit up again. Adding to the excitement was Marshmallow, zigzagging around us as fast as his short legs would carry him. Most of the time, he scooped lost Frisbees off the ground, but now and then he snagged a Frisbee on the fly, and when he did that, the crowd went wild.

I guess the whole thing looked pretty cool; there were oohs and aahs from the sidewalk everywhere we passed. By the time we reached the judging stand on College Street, the kids who took dance had added spins, while the ones who took martial arts had added kicks and punches.

Even Toby Lee, who is just little, was getting the hang of throwing the Frisbee. His mom, Marjie, looked up as if she was thanking heaven. "At last," she said, "the kid turns out to be good at something besides making a mess."

The parade route went south on Main Street, circled the campus, and ended near the north football parking lots—the really big ones at the edge of campus.

By the time we got there, we were almost as sick of "Baby Elephant Walk" as we were of the Twelve Days song.

CHAPTER TWENTY-SEVEN

The band members put their instruments down, and Toby Lee looked up at his mom. "Aw ovah?" he said sadly.

"All over." His mom nodded. "But wasn't that fun? And now there are awards! Come on and let's see if we won."

The Ice Carnival people had set up a platform at the far end of the parking lot. Mr. Glassie stood on it and one by one thanked almost every person in the entire town for making the first annual Ice Carnival Costume Pet Parade possible.

Boring!

Plus it took forever, and during it a lot of people left, including Mrs. Henry and Sophie's mom, who took Byron with her. I told them *no problemo,* my parents could give Sophie and Eve a ride home—even though I hadn't actually seen either of my parents yet.

Then it was time for the awards, and guess who gave them out: Mrs. Miggins!

A basset hound wearing a firefighter's hat and

a red plastic garbage bag (it was supposed to look like a coat) won the ribbon for best costume. The runner-up was a beagle ballerina that had a crown and some foofy pink fabric like a tutu around its belly.

"The pet costumes in California were better," Eve whispered.

"I heard that," Sophie said.

"Give 'em a break, Eve," I said. "They only had a day!"

We were part of the team division, which was won by six guys who live over in the Fairmount neighborhood. They had parrots on their shoulders and were pushing lawn mowers decorated with Christmas lights. I was a little disappointed until Mr. Glassie announced "the last award of the evening, a people's choice award, to the Chickadee Court Precision Light-Up Frisbee Team!" Then he explained that the idea for the parade had come from Sophie, Eve, and me, and cheers erupted all around.

We collected our red ribbons from Mrs. Miggins—Toby Lee grinned like crazy—and after that, it was time to go home.

But where were Mom and Dad? Had Luau's vet appointment taken such a really long time? Suddenly, I felt guilty because in all the excitement, I had forgotten about my sick cat.

"Sophie, can you check your phone?" I said. "My dad didn't call you, did he?"

Sophie checked and shook her head. No calls. Then she tried to call my dad, but he didn't pick up. Meanwhile, the stadium parking lot began to empty out.

"I say we wait ten minutes, then call my mom," I said.

The three of us went over to the speakers' platform and sat down on the edge. Eve hadn't heard Jeremiah talking to Billy before the parade, so Sophie and I caught her up. Meanwhile, Marshmallow was dozing in Eve's lap. He was one tired little Frisbee dog.

"So Billy and Jeremiah must've moved the lady dancing over to the unfinished house. That's how they got the splinters," Eve said.

"*Duh,*" said Sophie.

"But why would they do that, do you think?" I asked.

"Yasmeen put them up to it," Eve said. "She doesn't like me."

This was true. But I didn't see what it had to do with hiding a lady dancing. Unless...

"You guys," I said, "right before Eve got the call telling us to go to the unfinished house, I was at Yasmeen's, right? And she was acting snotty, and I said we were going to solve the case any minute. Okay, I guess I was acting a little snotty, too. So what if she heard that and decided to do something to keep it from happening?"

Sophie nodded. "Like sending us on a wild-goose chase, you mean. Eve, could it have been Yasmeen on the phone?"

Eve shrugged. "Maybe. I've only talked to her that time at the Jensens' disaster party. If it was her, though, it was a rotten thing to do."

Eve was right, but Yasmeen had been my friend so long, I had to defend her. "Except for the splinters, no harm was really done."

"It's kind of funny if she did it because she thought we were close to solving the case," Sophie said, "because actually, we're not."

Eve looked up. She had that scrunched-face look again. "You're wrong. We're very close to solving it." Then she clipped Marshmallow's leash to his collar, set him on the ground, stood up, and said, "Come on."

CHAPTER TWENTY-EIGHT

Eve walked so fast that Sophie and I had to jog and Marshmallow practically had to gallop. What was going on? If we were about to solve the case, I should be happy. But instead I was more like freaked because Eve seemed so upset.

Sophie said, "What is the matter with you, anyway, Eve? Where are we going?"

"Way to show sympathy, Soph," I said.

Eve ignored all this, but when I said, "You've gotta stop for a second. Marshmallow's exhausted," she did stop—just long enough for me to bend down, undo his leash, and pick him up. Then she strode off again.

We had left the stadium behind and now, across the lawn ahead of us, I saw three buildings. The closest one was a big metal warehouse. Maybe it was the moonlit silver clouds in the background, but it made me think of a spaceship in a science fiction movie. Then, as we got nearer, I heard a mechanical hum, sort of like our new refrigerator—the big one Dad got when he started the pie business.

Wait a sec. A refrigerator? This was RSF-Z, the refrigerated facility where Al was making all the deliveries. In the car, Eve's mom had said it would be a perfect place to store ice sculptures.

Oh. My. Gosh.

Did Eve really think the ice sculptures were there? Had she been thinking all along that it was her dad who had them? But that made no sense.

We were closing in on the storage building when Marshmallow raised his head, sniffed the air, and yipped: *I don't like this. I don't like this. Something just smells wrong.*

Then he wiggled so hard I couldn't hold him, and jumped to the ground. I figured his plan was to run away, but instead he ran toward the building and started sniffing the weeds around it. To our right was a red door with a sign: DANGER. KEEP OUT.

Eve, being a sensible person, stopped when she got to the red door. "What do we do?"

Sophie, on the other hand, didn't stop at all. She put her hand on the doorknob, tried to turn it, and...succeeded.

What was it doing unlocked, anyway?

"Sophie"—I grabbed her shoulder—"if the statues are in there, there might be bad guys. They might have weapons."

"Oh, hogwash," said Sophie. "Who cares enough about ice to guard it with a weapon?"

"Uh…maybe the same people who cared enough to steal ice in the first place?"

This slowed her down, but only for a second. "How do we even know ice is what's in there?"

Eve said, "I think it's ice. I think all along it was my dad who stole the sculptures. Remember the pickup truck? And the sunflower seeds? It's been so crazy for him lately, he probably started chewing them again. Not to mention he's got a zillion graduate students who would help him do whatever he told them to do—like steal every ice sculpture in town. Besides that, he was gone all night—remember? He told Mom and me he was in his lab, but maybe…"

I took a breath, let it out, and nodded. "Means and opportunity. But what about motive?"

Eve looked really sad. "I have no idea."

"Come on, you guys." Sophie pushed the door open. "Maybe the clue we need's in here."

I don't need to tell you it was pitch-black in the warehouse.

It's always pitch-black in a warehouse.

Waiting for my eyes to adjust, I thought of every

good old-fashioned mystery novel I'd ever read—where the eager detective goes in blind and ends up thumped on the head.

Then, at the start of the next chapter, he (or she) wakes up gagged, confused, and suffering from a bad, bad headache.

CHAPTER TWENTY-NINE

Remind me to give Sophie some good old-fashioned mystery novels for her birthday—because the way it turned out, going into the pitch-black warehouse was just as bad an idea as I expected.

Right away it was obvious that the darkness was populated with something, because I banged into obstacles everywhere I turned. Then, as if we needed something more to worry about, Marshmallow howled and started barking. *Danger! Danger! Danger!*

It didn't take special skill to know what he meant: Someone was in here in the dark with us!

My heart pounded, my hands shook, my stomach twisted itself in a knot.

In comparison, a mere thump on the head was looking good.

"*Ow!*" Sophie griped, then "*Ow!*" and "*Ow—my toe!*" and then she said some words she must have learned from cable. "We need a lantern," she added. "My phone doesn't throw enough light. Wait…—I wonder…" And then there was a strcak of light sailing near the ceiling of the warehouse, and for a shining moment we could see.

And what we saw were ice sculptures, rows of them lined up like zombies, staring blindly ahead in the Frisbee's light. The one I had just kicked was the zombified Ice Eve herself, and next to her an Ice Santa Claus, and then the chef with the tray of pizza, and then...the Frisbee hit the far wall—*thwack*—and bounced off, and everything went dark.

The thing is, it wasn't only ice sculptures I had seen in the moment of light. Unless I was crazy, something had moved, something like a purple shadow. And it made me remember how when I was downtown, I'd thought I was being followed. That was something purple, too. And hadn't there been something purple in the unfinished house?

Marshmallow barked again, then ran to retrieve Sophie's Frisbee. I could hear his doggy toenails *click-clicket*ing like crazy across the concrete floor.

Meanwhile, I took my own Frisbee and tossed it gently—going for maximum hang time and maximum light. Now the whole warehouse lit up, and we could see the sculptures more clearly, their faces distorted and scary because each had melted a bit in its day in the sun.

This was just great. Glowing, spooky, half-melted,

unseeing, zombie-like ice goblins. I already knew they would populate my nightmares for the rest of my life.

Marshmallow brought back my Frisbee, brought back Eve's Frisbee, brought back Sophie's for the second time. For a scared little dog, he was tough. Now we tossed them as soon as they came back, so that they rose above the sculptures one after another, then sometimes—*oops*—collided in midair and dropped to the floor.

Not to mention, they bounced off the ice sculptures, too…

…Which was when something strange happened—sparks, like you'd get from striking a match, followed by what looked like tiny bolts of lightning. At first I thought they were just reflections from the spinning light-up Frisbees, but then I saw that they were different, multicolored.

"Never saw ice act like that before," said Sophie.

"Me nei—" I started to say, but then I saw, streaking from the place where a Frisbee had just fallen, a whole bunch of lightning sparks—*poof-poof-poof*—a chain reaction that spawned a star of linked lightning, accompanied by poofs and hisses and pops, and that was spreading outward fast.

Sophie said, "Huh."

Eve said, "I don't like the looks of this."

Then the hisses and pops got louder, and the lightning sparks brightened and multiplied.

What did *volatile* mean again? Suddenly, it came to me: *Might blow up*—that's what it meant!

"You guys, we've got to get out of here!"

Eve, Sophie, and I started backing toward the door. "Marshmallow?" I called. "Come on!"

By now the whole room was brightening, with all the nightmare ice sculptures on view. Weirdly, it seemed to be the ice itself producing the lightning effect, kind of like...

Wait a second.

The video clip of the flame coming out of the faucet? The *poof* when Uncle Jim disappeared from the video conference—he had been turning on a faucet, right?

Had Uncle Jim made the ice sculptures out of water from Belleburg?

CHAPTER THIRTY

There's nothing like a healthy shot of adrenaline to power up the brain. As Eve, Sophie, and I backpedaled toward the warehouse door, I started to work the mystery out.

It was never the ice at all that the thief wanted.

It was the water!

Mr. Yoder had made his ice sculptures from the water that came out of his tap—water polluted by fracking. And Professor Henry must have figured out that one of the chemicals polluting the water could be used as the missing ingredient he needed to make grassoline.

It made a crazy kind of sense. Hadn't Professor Olivo said the catalyzing agent was volatile? Unfortunately, now the pulsing bolts of lightning made the warehouse bright as day and raised the temperature inside, too.

"Marshmallow!" Eve called.

And there he was, at last—maneuvering like a tiny, fluffy running back among the dripping figures—then, *zoom*, he was out the door. Meanwhile the *sizzle-crackle-poof* had become one thunderous rumble, and the steamy air felt quivery and electric.

Something was about to happen, something big and dangerous.

Eve, Sophie, and I had reached the door and were about to cross the threshold to safety when, on the far side of the warehouse, I saw something purple and human-sized. It was familiar not only because it had been following me all day…but also because it was my best friend.

What was Yasmeen doing here?

More importantly—how was she going to get out?

With Eve and Sophie safe outside, I reversed direction. By now, the air in the warehouse was warm and sticky, the light had gone from bright to blinding, and the concrete floor was slick with melting ice. Out of breath, I slid and stumbled forward, tripping on the shrunken remains of Mr. Yoder's sculptures. Suddenly—behind me—someone screamed my name, grabbed me around the waist, and dragged me toward the door.

I fought back. I couldn't leave Yasmeen!

But whoever had me in his or her grip had almost superhuman strength. A few seconds later, I was outside in the dark, breathing gulps of cold night air.

"Run, Alex! Run away *now!*" yelled a very familiar voice—and I knew arguing would be useless.

It always is with Mom.

So I did as I was told.

And Mom rushed back inside to get Yasmeen.

CHAPTER THIRTY-ONE

When I turned my back on the warehouse, I saw Sophie, Eve, and Marshmallow at the edge of the lawn. The girls were waving, and I ran toward them. By now I could hear sirens, and soon there were blinking red and white lights coming toward us from the road in the distance.

I reached the girls. The three of us turned to look at RSF-Z. Then we waited breathlessly for whatever was going to happen next. It didn't take long. There was a flash of multicolored light and a *whoosh-bang* roar that drove a single shock wave, knocking us backward. Marshmallow—huddled in Eve's arms—howled. A blizzard wind kicked up, frigid with the vaporized remains of ice sculptures. It left a layer of icy white on the ground and on us.

I wiped my eyes. I realized I was crying.

Where was Yasmeen?

And where was my mom?

The noise echoed in my skull for several seconds; then it got eerily quiet; then I heard the sirens again. Within moments, police cars screamed up, then a fire engine, and after that two ambulances. Eve, Sophie, and I watched speechlessly while the emergency workers poured out of their vehicles, shone spotlights on the wrecked building, and put up barriers and yellow police tape to seal off the area.

Within a few minutes, the fire guys had suited up and swarmed the wreckage. In all the chaos, it was hard to see exactly what was happening, but eventually the EMS people pulled two backboards out of the ambulance.

"What are they doing now?" Eve asked.

"They've got patients," Sophie said.

"Come on," I said, and we headed for the emergency vehicles and what was left of RSF-Z.

Approaching the taped-off boundary, we saw Officer Krichels, who put up his hands to say *Stop.* "Hi, kids. Now, you know I can't let you come any closer. It's too dangerous, and we've got our work to do."

"Is my mom—?" I tried to ask. "Yasmeen—?"

Officer Krichels looked really serious. "They're going to the hospital," he said, "and that's all I can tell you 'cause that's all I know."

Suddenly Bub was there—he had come up behind me.

And I was never so glad to see anyone in my life.

"I've called your dad, Alex, and Yasmeen's parents," he said. "They'll meet us at the hospital. Your parents are coming, too, girls. Hop in my truck and let's go."

Lying on beds in the hospital's emergency room, Mom and Yasmeen both looked terrible. They had braces around their necks. Their faces were pink-splotched and scratched. They were hooked up to beeping machines that read their heartbeats and blood pressure. Hanging from metal poles next to their beds were bags of clear liquid connected by tubes to their bandaged arms. The doctor explained there was medicine in the liquid to kill germs, replace fluids, and help them sleep.

It was scary seeing them that way. But they were alive. I tried to concentrate on that.

"Detective Parakeet's body has had a severe shock, and we won't know about the extent of her internal injuries for a while," the doctor explained to my dad and me as we stood by her. "Luckily, the burns seem to be superficial."

Only a green curtain separated Mom's bed from Yasmeen's, and I could hear Yasmeen trying to say something. Her parents were in the hall talking to a nurse, so I went around and bent down next to her. "What, Yasmeen? Can I get you anything?"

"Unh-unh," she croaked, and I could barely hear her. "I just wanted to tell you…that *superficial*…means…not deep."

I reported this conversation to Sophie, Eve, and Bub a couple of minutes later. They were in the waiting area outside the emergency room.

Bub tried to laugh, but it came out like more of a sob. "Now I know"—he wiped his eyes—"she'll be okay."

A few minutes after that, Professor Henry arrived, no longer looking anything like the confident scientist from the Jensens' disaster party. Instead, he looked sad and uncertain. When he tried to give Eve a hug, she pulled away.

My dad came into the waiting room at almost the same moment. The doctor was getting my mom ready to move her upstairs. We could go see her in her own hospital room later.

Compared to Professor Henry, my dad—proprietor of Pie in the Sky Pies—looked totally intimidating.

"Well?" was my dad's greeting. "What do you have to say for yourself?"

Professor Henry sighed. "'I'm sorry' is inadequate."

"It would be a start, though," Dad said. "And after that—how about if you admit responsibility?"

"I am sorry," Professor Henry said, "from the bottom of my heart. And I won't make excuses for myself. This dream of mine—grassoline—has overcome my good sense and my moral sense, too. I see that, after what's happened tonight. I only hope the damage isn't permanent. Your wife? Ms. Popp? How are they?"

"The doctors don't know yet," Dad said. "They're doing tests and will assess again in the morning."

Before Professor Henry could reply to that, Sophie cut him off. "I've got some questions for you."

"Sophie," I said, "at this point, shouldn't we let the police—?"

"What police?" Sophie said. "Your mom's not going to be doing a whole lot of detecting for a while yet. I say we help her out."

Professor Henry smiled grimly. "I don't mind answering your questions, uh—what's your name, again?"

Sophie put out her hand. "Sophie Sikora. And this is Alex Parakeet. We're your neighbors on Chickadee Court. And I guess you remember your daughter—even though you hardly ever have time for her. We've been investigating. The first thing I want to know is, when did you start chewing sunflower seeds again?"

Dad and I looked at Sophie like, *Wha'?* But Eve

giggled, which was a pleasant sound under the circumstances.

"How did you know about that?" Professor Henry asked. "Never mind—it doesn't matter. Probably a month ago, right before we moved. I was under a lot of stress. But I had to do it in secret because my wife doesn't approve."

"Maybe, if you don't mind, you could back up a little," I said. "What was your plan, exactly? I mean, I figured out there's a volatile chemical in the fracking liquid, a chemical you think will work as a catalyst for making grassoline, so you had it frozen into ice sculptures."

Professor Henry looked surprised. "My wife told me about your reputation as a detective, Alex. I see it's deserved." He took a breath. "Well, all right. I may as well explain it all. The plan was to transfer the sculptures to RSF-Z after Ice Carnival ended. But then the weather forecast called for warming. I was terrified they might melt. And if they did—"

"*Ka-boom!*" Sophie threw her hands in the air.

"Uh, yes. Basically," said Professor Henry. "So my students and I gathered the sculptures from downtown in the dead of night. I knew I could count on them to keep quiet about it. And then I went over to Chickadee Court in my old truck and collected Eve myself."

"By 'gather them up,' you mean you stole them, right, dear?" Mrs. Henry had come in from the parking lot.

"It was in the best interests of science, not to mention the environment," Professor Henry insisted. "Grassoline—"

Mrs. Henry cut him off. "Grassoline is not going to do a thing for Yasmeen or Detective Parakeet."

Professor Henry hung his head, and there was an uncomfortable silence.

Bub broke it. "What you're saying, Professor, puts me in mind of something my friend Al told us the other day. He mentioned how it's pretty near impossible to get a permit from the state for hauling explosives."

Professor Henry nodded. "That's right, and that's why I was forced to enlist my brother-in-law's help to hide the chemical in ice sculptures."

"Uncle Jim was in on this?" Eve said.

Professor Henry nodded. "He thought finding a use for dirty fracking water would be good for everyone in the end. Besides that, I promised him a share of the proceeds from grassoline. Anyway, we didn't have time to wait for state permits if we were going to be the first to market with our product. The competing team from my old university has been hot on our heels."

So Sophie was right, I thought, *in a way.* The motive was money. Professor Henry wanted his kind of grassoline to win the race—because if it did, he and Mr. Yoder and the college and a lot of other people would make a ton of money.

I remembered something else, too. Hadn't my mom's annoying tipster—the one who turned out to be Professor Olivo—warned about "poison bombs on the highway"? So he wasn't crazy! He knew Professor Henry was looking for a *volatile* catalyzing chemical, and he was afraid Professor Henry might be willing to take a chance and transport it illegally, too.

A nurse appeared at the emergency room door. "Which one of you is Alex? Could you come back a moment?"

I figured it was Mom who wanted something, but it was Yasmeen. This time she was sitting up. Her parents were standing beside her cot. They nodded hello to me but never took their eyes off their daughter.

"Alex," Yasmeen whispered. "I have to tell you something."

"Oh, honey," said Mrs. Popp. "Don't tire yourself out."

"It's important." Yasmeen tried to shake her head but couldn't because of the brace around her neck.

She couldn't open her mouth very wide, either, which made her hard to understand. "My brain's all fuzzy—or I would've thought of it sooner. It's about Luau. Is he okay?"

Oh my gosh, I had totally forgotten my cat! "I don't know. He was acting strange. Dad took him to the vet, but that was before—"

"Alex, listen," Yasmeen interrupted, and the rest came out in breathless gasps: "Luau might be sick. I took him over to the Henrys' front yard today. I needed him to keep Marshmallow out of the way while I looked for clues. When we were there—he drank some of the melted ice…from where Ice Eve was standing? I didn't think anything about it till tonight when I saw that the sculptures weren't made out of plain water. Alex, listen. You have to find out if your cat's been poisoned."

CHAPTER THIRTY-TWO

I didn't sleep that night.

Except I guess I must have. Because otherwise, how come I woke up the next morning?

It was New Year's Day, Eve's birthday, the first day of the year—the worst day of my life.

Luau wasn't sitting on my chest or swishing his tail in my face the way he should have been. He was at the vet's, and the vet couldn't promise he'd ever come home.

My mom was in the hospital.

My best friend was in the hospital.

Along with Sophie and Eve, I had solved a mystery—but I didn't feel good about it. How could I feel good when my new friend's dad would probably have to go to jail?

I washed and got dressed and went downstairs and played video games. Dad knew how I was feeling and didn't even bug me to do anything useful. He just came in, said hello, and left me alone. The plan was to go to the hospital after lunch. That was when the doctors were going to decide about Mom and Yasmeen coming home.

At eleven o'clock the phone rang, and Dad picked it up in the kitchen. Was it the vet? I went to find out.

"Mr. Parakeet, yes," Dad was saying, "and don't tell me because I know it's a funny name for a cat owner. How is Luau doing?"

For a few moments, Dad's face didn't give anything away. He just listened and nodded and then—*finally*—he smiled and gave me a thumbs-up. I didn't even realize I'd been holding my breath till I grabbed a gulp of air so big it made me cough.

Luau was going to be okay!

In the car on the way to get him, Dad told me what the vet had said. It turned out to be lucky Yasmeen had told me when she did about Luau drinking the ice-melt. The chemical in the melted ice smells good to dogs and cats, but in their bodies it acts a lot like antifreeze, the stuff you put in cars. Pets drink antifreeze sometimes because it's sweet, but it's also deadly poison if you don't act fast.

"Hey, guy—how ya feeling?" I picked Luau up off the table in the vet's examining room. When I held him close, he clutched me with his claws. *Alex, get me out of here. There's not a comfy cushion in the place.*

Luau wasn't the only one who got to go home that day. So did Mom, and so did Yasmeen. The doctors said they had been lucky, too, and their injuries weren't severe. Neither one of them could remember exactly what had happened, but they must have been clear of the warehouse before the blast.

I spent the rest of the day nursing patients, and I didn't mind at all.

My mom was what's known as a good patient. She liked staying in bed with a book and having Dad and me bring her tea. She worried that the cuts on her face might scar, and she didn't like aching all over, but otherwise she said it was like a vacation. She also said thank you a lot.

The only bad part was she kept mussing up my hair the way I hate.

Yasmeen and Luau, on the other hand, were terrible patients.

Luau, being a cat, was happy to lie around 99 percent motionless. But he was 100 percent full of complaints. The pillow was lumpy. The sun was in his eyes. His medicine tasted awful. He was extra-grumpy because before we left, the vet had said he should go back on a diet—no more kitty treats.

Then there was Yasmeen. She couldn't stand to

stay still. Her mom had to threaten to tie her down.

"And the piano is definitely off-limits," Mrs. Popp said.

Jeremiah was delighted about that last part. "You heard Mom," he said. "'Definitely off-limits.'"

"Go away," Yasmeen told Jeremiah. "Please."

She was on the sofa in the den. I was sitting next to her in a chair. Everything hurt, she said, and she didn't feel like reading or watching TV.

"Do you feel like talking?" I asked.

"No," she said. "But what?"

"There're still some things about the case I don't get," I said. "Like were you following me yesterday when I was downtown?"

"Not exactly following," she said. "I think I actually went downtown before you did. I talked to Tim Roberts."

"Wait...what?" So that was why he hadn't said, "Where's Yasmeen?" He'd known where she was. She had already been there.

"I wanted to solve the case as much as you did, bud. Maybe even more, because I wanted to show I'm better than your new best friend, Eve."

I let that last part go for the moment. "Hey... and did you talk to Coach Hathaway, too?"

Yasmeen nodded. "I ran into him when I was out looking for clues."

"Did you find the sunflower crud?"

Yasmeen made a face. "Sunflower crud?"

Ha! Score one for Alex Parakeet. "I'll tell you about it later. Then did you go to the unfinished house?"

"I did," she said. "I know that part was stupid, and I'm sorry, but I was so mad at you—mad at everybody, I guess. Anyway, I wanted to make sure Jeremiah and Billy had moved the lady dancing like I asked them to. Only I slipped and knocked over some boards and made a lot of noise."

"And later you went out to RSF-Z," I said.

Yasmeen nodded. "With your mom."

"*What?!*"

"I knew the ice sculptures had to be at Professor Henry's lab complex. I mean, where else would he have hidden them?"

"Wait a second," I said. "You knew Professor Henry stole the ice sculptures?"

"*Duh*, Alex."

"I don't get it. How—?"

Yasmeen reached over and picked up a book, *The Memoirs of Sherlock Holmes*, from the table next to the sofa. "It's all here in a story called 'Silver Blaze.' The clue that incriminates the murderer is a dog that doesn't bark. This was the same situation. Marshmallow barks if a snowflake even hits the ground, but he didn't bark when Ice Eve was stolen in the middle of the night. I wondered why not, and then I remembered that in the story, it's the dog's owner that's the bad guy. In this case, the answer was the same. If the thief wasn't an intruder, it basically had to be Professor Henry."

I couldn't believe it. "I should have just asked Marshmallow!" I said.

Yasmeen sighed. "Alex? You're not going to tell me you can talk to Marshmallow, are you?"

I shook my head. "Of course not," I said. "I would never tell you that. But go back a second. What about my mom?"

"I would have been stupid to confront Professor Henry on my own, wouldn't I? I needed reinforcements, so I called your mom, and she went with me. It's useful to have a police officer around, bud. For example, she had a gizmo on her belt that opened the door to the warehouse."

"So *that's* why the door was unlocked! But she wasn't inside when Eve and Sophie and I arrived, was she?"

"She was at her car getting a lantern," Yasmeen said, "and I guess calling in reinforcements, too. She didn't realize how dangerous it was in the warehouse."

I was getting ready to go home and check my

other patients when the phone rang in another room and Mrs. Popp came in, holding out the receiver for Yasmeen.

"It's okay with me," Mrs. Popp told Yasmeen, "if you feel up to it."

When Yasmeen was done, she handed the phone to me.

"Alex?" It was Eve. In spite of all that had happened, she wanted to have a small party to celebrate her birthday. Could I come over later?

I looked at Yasmeen and she nodded—she was going, so I said I would, too.

"It's gonna be tough for Eve now with her dad in trouble," Yasmeen explained after I had hung up. "I mean, she'll probably have to go back to California. So—the least we can do is be nice the last few days she's around."

Nobody would blame me if I called Eve's birthday another disaster party.

On the other hand, before the bad part happened, Eve told me something amazing: Professor Olivo had talked to the district attorney and convinced him to keep both Professor Henry and her uncle Jim out of jail!

Say what?

"Crazy, huh?" Eve said. Like you can imagine, she had a huge grin on her face. "But Professor Olivo figured out it would be good if they could all work together instead of hating each other, since he—Professor Olivo—is interested in fracking and Dad needs the chemical from fracking water to make his grassoline."

Yasmeen nodded. "That makes a lot of sense." The three of us were on the sofa in the basement, where Mrs. Henry had set up games and party food, which—since the Henrys are from California—included guacamole. "And since your dad and your uncle can't exactly work from jail, they'll probably stay out."

Eve said, "It's even possible that if Dad pays back the Ice Carnival and pays to rebuild RSF-Z, the judge will go easy on him."

"So...," Yasmeen said. "You might not have to go back to California?"

Eve grinned. "Yeah, you might be stuck with me awhile."

"Cool!" said Sophie Sikora, who was listening in as usual.

The disaster part happened when we sang "Happy Birthday." Yasmeen was singing her heart out. Eve didn't even crack a smile, but Toby Lee is just a bad little kid. My dad had sent over another chocolate cream pie, and Toby picked it up and aimed it at Yasmeen. I knew what a good arm he had with a light-up Frisbee, so I moved to block his throw, and…succeeded.

I blocked it with my face.

Faster than you can say "Three Stooges"—all that singing turned to laughter.

It was Yasmeen who recovered first. "Here, Alex, I'll help you clean up."

Then Eve said, "It's my party. I'll help him."

And I said, "Sheesh, you guys, you don't have to fight over me."

For a second, it was quiet; then Yasmeen and Eve together said, *"Ewww!"* and next thing you know I was in the bathroom cleaning up my own face.

Looking in the mirror, I realized something. The mystery of who stole New Year's Eve had been solved. But the mystery of girls was going to take a little longer.